ABOUT THE AUTHOR

Orchard Books
338 Euston Road
London NW1 3BH

Orchard Books Australia
Level 17/207 Kent Street
Sydney, NSW 2000

First published in Great Britain in 2007
A paperback original
ISBN 978 1 84616 621 1
Text c Michael Lawrence 2007
The right of Michael Lawrence to be identified as the author of this work has been asserted
by him in accordance with the Copyrights, Designs and Patents Act, 1988
All rights reserved
A CIP catalogue record for this book is available from the British Library
10 9 8 7 6 5 4 3 2 1
Printed in Great Britain

Orchard Books is a division of Hachette Children's Books, an Hachette Livre UK company
www.orchardbooks.co.uk

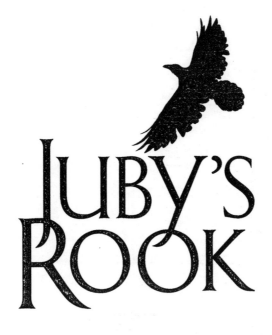

JUBY'S ROOK

MICHAEL LAWRENCE

ORCHARD BOOKS

This book is for Cindy, who is so fond of the story and was there at the beginning of it, and Abi, who walked the high cliffs at 'Crowbarrow' with me one sweltering August day to see if a wheezy old codger could survive such a trek (I did, but only just).

AUTHOR'S NOTE

The action of this novel takes place in and around a real village in the south-west of England whose fate, as described here, was its true one. I have not used its true name, however, calling it Rouklye (pronounced Rooklee), because I felt more comfortable writing within that small fiction. I have also changed the name of a nearby coastal hamlet, but the names of several other places and landmarks in the vicinity have been retained.

Here as I take my solitary rounds,
Amidst thy tangling walks and ruined grounds,
And, many a year elapsed, return to view
Where once the cottage stood, the hawthorn grew,
Remembrance wakes with all her busy train,
Swells at my breast, and turns the past to pain.

From *The Deserted Village* by Oliver Goldsmith

ONE

It was the last year of the old century, and Midge Miller hadn't smiled for a week. She was fifteen and bored out of her mind: away from home, friends, everything she knew, liked, owned, in the dullest backwater imaginable. There wasn't even a TV in her room. Wasn't a TV in the entire crummy house. Yet even here, in this mood, she couldn't help a small laugh at the sight from her window above the bookshop. The gangling old man who'd parked outside the inn across the road had just struggled out of his prehistoric Volkswagen, and, straightening up, revealed that he was one of the tallest men she'd ever seen, which made his car seem one of the smallest.

'Juby!'

She jumped – hadn't heard the floorboards – and before she could turn, Inger was crouching at her shoulder, also peering out.

'I was beginning to wonder if he was going to give this year a miss. He's usually here before the second week if he's coming. Must be slowing up at last. Or do I mean down, I can never remember.'

'You know him?' Midge said.

'Oh, yes. An old, old friend. And he and Edwin were boys together. Juby comes over every August from Germany to prowl round childhood haunts.'

'Germany?'

'He lives there. In Wiesbaden. He could stay here when he visits, but him and Edwin – tuh! The tension when they're together, you could cut it with scissors.'

They watched the incredibly tall man lean into the car for the jacket that matched his sagging black trousers. As he attempted to put the jacket on, all arms and elbows that seemed uncertain which way to go, Inger rose from her crouch.

'What I came up for,' she said, 'was to ask if you're helping in the shop again today.'

Midge stiffened. Placed the thumb and fingertips of one hand on the window glass. Five tense digits. The other five a claw at her side. It was like being at home.

You always had to be *doing* something. Couldn't just sit at a window minding your own business, oh no. Criminal offence, looking out of a window.

'If you like.'

'It's not compulsory,' Inger said with the kind of edge she usually reserved for Edwin.

Midge let her hand fall from the glass; tried to sound less fed up.

'No. Really. I don't mind.'

'When you're ready then. No rush.'

Then she was alone again, watching the ungainly old man negotiate the doorway of The Ferryman. To pass through the entrance – low even for people of normal height – he had to drop his head to shoulder level, but as his shoulders were higher than the top of most men's heads he still managed to crack his skull. Again she laughed. Woh, two laughs in two minutes. A laugh a minute, have to watch that, people will think being abandoned by your parents is fun.

Abandoned. Well, it felt like it. Most of the time her parents shuffled papers at the *Earthsave International* offices in Worcester, but every now and then some big threat to humanity would crop up somewhere in the world and they'd be off with a boatload of other superheroes to try and prevent it, frustrate it, or aggravate its perpetrators.

This time it was some lunatic dictatorship (the Inanians, Dad called them) testing their latest weapon of mass destruction in the South Pacific. The long-promised trip to Orlando had been scrapped and they'd cast about for somewhere to leave her in a hurry. Usually when they went on these missions she was left with Nessa and her parents, but the Friedmans had gone away a couple of days before the Inanian thing came up, which reduced the alternatives to one: her grandparents in South Dorset.

She turned angrily from the window, into the gloomy little cell she'd been sentenced to for the best month of the year. Angrily because her parents made it plain (if not in so many words) that they thought more of others than of her. Didn't they realise how unsettling this knowledge was? That their selfless efforts to protect the planet at her expense were the real reason her school work was suffering? She'd tried telling them this, but she always came badly out of such confrontations. Compared with their brazen humanitarian objectives, her pitiful attempts to present her case made her sound like a self-centred brat.

'If no one reacted against such things, Midge, the world would be right up shit creek.'

'It *is* up shit creek, you're always saying.'

'Yes, but someone has to try to make things better.'

'Well, why can't it be someone *else*?'

'If we all said that, darling, nothing would ever improve.'

The end result of which was that she 'must be strong' and look beyond her 'own domestic preferences': arguments she had no option but to submit to.

She wondered how Nessa would handle such parents. Better than her, no doubt. Nessa handled everything better. As well as enviably good looks and effortless charm, she could express herself concisely and tellingly and was good at everything she wanted to be good at – on top of which the boys only had eyes for her when the two of them were out together. She sometimes wondered why Ness bothered with her. Probably for no other reason than that they were next-door neighbours and had known one another for ever. Another year or so and she was bound to move on, find friends more like herself – attractive, quick-witted, mistress of any situation – while she, Midge, would continue to be condemned to cells like this because...

She dashed an arm across her eyes and allowed them a watery inspection of the room she'd been so unceremoniously dumped in. What a hovel. No carpet, just a big square rug on bare brown boards: a thin faded thing with unravelling ends that she longed to tug till there was nothing left. Ornaments included an ancient jug-and-bowl set (bowl cracked, jug the last resting place of a dead spider), a pair of dusty Staffordshire dogs, ugly fragments of rock on every flat surface, a wooden chess set with a piece missing. On the walls, in thin black frames, there were a couple of dozen old photos that held no interest whatsoever. The pictures were wonky, all of them, and wonky they would stay. Nothing to do with her. Inger had attempted to make the room more welcoming by placing – side-by-side on the huge, badly-scuffed Edwardian chest of drawers – a pensionable china doll from someone else's childhood and a one-eyed bear (with stuffing leaking out of its bottom) that might have been found on a council tip. Midge could take or leave the doll, but she'd hated the bear on sight and turned it to the wall so its single staring eye couldn't watch her getting undressed. You never knew what went on in these old bears' moth-eaten minds.

Then there was the mirror: a creaky, full-length mahogany chevalier which seemed to catch her reflection wherever she went about the room. It was her general practice to avoid mirrors as much as she could. The obligatory peek before going out was rarely more than that; just a glance to make sure there was no sleep in her eyes, food lodged between her teeth, that her hair was reasonably tidy, and so on. Mirrors were a curse. They revealed what everyone saw when they looked at her: gawky frame, too-wide shoulders, big nose, patchy complexion prone to spottiness, hair like tangled rope if she didn't wash it daily. If she didn't look quite as bad in the chevalier, it wasn't because its old specked glass possessed some special quality or power, it was merely that it was slightly darker than the mirrors she was used to, and reflected a different arrangement of light and shade than more familiar rooms. Maybe the girl in the mirror is the real Midge, she thought sardonically. The Midge in the mirror smiled. Clearly she'd been thinking that too.

Then they both turned, one to the left, one to the right, and went out to their separate landings, where at least one smile quickly faded. Midge couldn't speak for the real her in the mirror, but her day did not look promising. She might have viewed it with more optimism – or at least more interest – if she'd known that it would be a day that would reshape her life. Set the wheels in motion anyway.

And all without mirrors.

Two

Her grandparents, Inger Bjølstad and Edwin Underwood, had been together, unmarried, for over forty years. Inger in particular saw no point in marriage and insisted on her surname being used on all documents and communications. 'We're two separate people,' she said, 'two *single* people, and we'll be treated as such.' Almost every adult who knew them on anything approaching a personal basis called them by their first names. So did Midge, but only in her head. She'd known them all her life, yet felt that she knew them hardly at all. Visits to them or by them had never been frequent, so until now she'd spent very little time alone in their company. Without her parents there, they made her nervous, especially Inger, who could be quite spiky when crossed. Midge had witnessed her anger with Edwin and Mum a couple of times and hoped that she herself would never be on the receiving end of it. She loved the way her grandmother spoke, however. Her accent was slight, her English more precise than most English people's, but every now and then she would put a Scandinavian spin on a word that suddenly made her seem the most colourful person around. Which she probably was anyway in a hole like Steepridge.

Inger was removing the old display from the shop window to make way for a new one while Midge went from shelf to shelf putting newly-delivered titles in alphabetical order. She was helping out because she felt obliged to: a way of earning the keep she didn't want. She could think of any number of things she'd rather be doing. No. Correction. She couldn't think of one, here.

'Midge, we have a visitor!'

The shop door sprang back and the hyperactive brass bell drowned out the thud of forehead smacking lintel. The incredibly tall man's knees folded and he staggered in clutching his head, one leg trying to walk away from him. If he'd been a character in a comic he would have had a halo of stars whizzing round his head. Inger jumped back from the window and threw a chair under the graceless giant just in time to stop him crashing to the floor.

'Juby Bench, how many years have I had this shop?'

He groaned. 'Please, not a quiz, spare me, woman.'

'And how many times have you banged your head on that door?'

'Can't remember, it's all that banging me head on the door.'

He removed his hand from his forehead and looked at it. There was nothing in it, but on his brow there was a reversed OU where it had rushed at the embossed MIND YOUR HEAD above the door.

'Bloody country. Everything's so *low* here.'

'Sit quiet a moment,' Inger commanded.

'I thought I was.' He scowled about him. The shop interior must have seemed very dull after the brilliant light outside. He peered Midge's way through the comparative gloom. 'Who's that?'

'Midge,' Inger said. 'She's staying with us for a few weeks.'

'Midge?'

'Midge Miller, my granddaughter from Worcester. Midge, come and meet Mr Bench.'

'Juby,' the old man said. 'Just Juby.'

As she approached he raised his rump two inches off

the chair and extended a startlingly long arm. The wrist on the end of the startlingly long arm was like a dog's favourite bone, while the palm that swamped hers was as smooth as a piece of worn old leather that's been left out in the sun. The knobbly fingers closed lightly but firmly, jerked her hand up and down twice, and withdrew. Then Juby Bench sat back and studied her.

'There is a likeness. To you, not Eddie. Does she look like your girl?'

'She does a bit,' Inger said. 'Not the hair, but the height, the shoulders. She also has Malena's eyes. And nose, to some extent.'

'Don't talk to me about noses.'

Inger laughed. Obviously an old joke between them. His nose was not one you could ignore. Midge had always been self-conscious about her own, but hers was positively petite beside his great beak. His eyes had not left her. Very pale, those eyes, an almost luminous blue, as if lit from within. Unnerving, the way they examined her.

'Midge, was it?' he said.

'Yes.'

'Like the insect?'

'Lost none of your charm over the past year, I see,' Inger said to him.

He ignored this. 'Why would anyone call their daughter Midge?'

'It's a nickname.' Inger again.

'I repeat, why would anyone call their daughter Midge?'

'She was a very small toddler.'

'She's not a toddler now, or small.'

'Nicknames stick, Juby.'

'What's your given name?' he asked Midge.

'Evy,' said Inger.

He flashed her an annoyed glance. 'Doesn't the girl have a tongue?'

'You're making her uncomfortable, can't you see?'

'Me, making her uncomfortable?' To Midge: 'I'm not, am I?'

He was, but she wasn't going to admit it. 'No.'

'Midge,' he murmured, turning the name over in his mouth like a boiled sweet he wasn't sure about. He shook his head. 'Nah. Doesn't fit. Not the young lady I see before me. I'll call you Evy. Much better.'

'She might not want you to call her Evy,' Inger said.

The exceedingly pale eyes drilled a silent question into Midge's own. She shrugged off-handedly. She didn't care what he called her; just wished he'd stop looking at her that way.

18

'How's the head?' Inger asked their visitor, tactfully obliging him to release her granddaughter from his gimlet gaze.

'Oh, wonderful,' he replied. 'If it belonged to someone else.'

Midge escaped to her shelves while she had the chance. From there, watching the pair of them between and over books, she saw Inger reach out and touch the old man's unshaven cheek, very delicately, like someone attempting Braille for the first time.

'Why so late this year, old chap?' Almost a whisper.

'Am I?'

'You know it. You're usually here before now.'

'I was taken a bit poorly.'

'Oh? Nothing serious, I hope?'

'If it was, d'you think I'd tell you? You'd send me straight to bed with a thermometer and a bunch of grapes.'

'But you're staying to the end of the month?'

'Can't say.'

'You're not usually so vague.'

Juby Bench gripped his knees to ease himself upward. His joints creaked as he rose. On his feet, he was forced to stoop in that low room, the ceiling flattening his unruly shock of wiry grey hair. He settled his angular jaw on one shoulder and his lips moved as though preparing to pass words, but then clamped shut. His eyes cut across to Midge, who tried to look engrossed in her work. He wants to tell Gran something personal, she thought, but can't with me here – which made her feel very much in the way.

It wasn't that. It was nothing like that. But it would be several days before she discovered what was on Juby Bench's mind, and then she would be sworn to secrecy, unable to share it with anyone. Anyone at all.

Three

It was perhaps a slight overstatement to say that Midge hadn't smiled for a week. There had been the odd reluctant smirk; always her grandfather's doing. Edwin Underwood had a way of making a joke of things that even Midge, determined to appear displeased when eyes were upon her, found hard to resist. He was especially entertaining when taking off Inger in one of her outbursts at the posturings of some 'idiot politician' on the radio or some foolish enquiry in the shop. When Inger was at her most agitated Edwin would stand behind her mimicking her outrageously, flapping his arms, juggling his eyebrows, and when she whirled round suspecting something of the sort there he'd be examining his fingernails and humming quietly. He also seemed to find it impossible to walk across a room like a normal person. He had a whole menagerie of silly walks. Sometimes he did a duck waddle, sometimes a high-kicking ostrich, sometimes he plodded around like an elephant. He did voices too. In fact he rarely used his own when she was about. She had two favourites: the dive-bomber whine and the John-Wayne-with-a-hangover growl. Inger wasn't amused by any of this. She must have heard it all, seen it all, countless times over the years. But her irritation didn't bother Edwin. On the contrary, he seemed to revel in it.

Most days he was already in the kitchen when Midge went down for breakfast, but the first she saw of him that morning was around eleven, shortly after Juby Bench went back to The Ferryman. She was arranging special offers on a little bookcase beside the desk when she heard the back door open and close, followed by the thump of something weighty being dropped on the kitchen table. Then Edwin was ambling along the corridor and looking in.

'I'm back.'

Inger, putting the finishing touches to her window display, said: 'Have you been somewhere?'

'I've been fishing since dawn, dearest. You must have noticed I wasn't here.'

She looked at Midge, wide-eyed. 'I don't think we did, did we?'

Midge grunted non-committally.

'You'd have noticed if they found me floating face down in the river,' Edwin said.

Inger flashed him an overripe smile. 'Not necessarily.'

'Well, I've got our tea out here. Nice pair of ripe young perch. Fish pie tonight.'

'We'll look forward to it,' she said. 'Should be home by tea-time.'

He frowned. 'Going somewhere?'

'We are. Very soon.' Inger stepped back, appraising her handiwork. In a minute she would assess it from the street, the only view that really counted. 'Which means,' she said, 'that you must mind the shop.'

Edwin's look of horror was a picture. 'Me? No chance. Put up the closed sign, it's your business, I'm retired.'

Inger plunged her hands into the deep pockets of her salmon pink dungarees and turned to him with a studiedly patient air.

'Edwin.'

'Don't Edwin me,' he said. 'What did I sell the last time you left me in charge? One lousy picture postcard, and it wasn't even a local.'

'That was April, this is August. In August, with the

stock that's just come in, and my discounts, even you can't fail.'

Edwin sighed – and gave in. There could only be one winner in arguments between these two, it seemed to Midge. Same one every time.

'Where you off to anyway?'

'You don't want to know,' Inger said.

Which made him even more curious. 'Come on, where?'

'Picnic.'

'Picnic? Just the two of you?'

'And Juby.'

'Ju...?' He took a long breath. 'When did he turn up?' His voice had gone quite cold.

'Checked in across the road a couple of hours ago.'

'Damn the man. I was going over there for a bite.'

'Well, you'll be able to when we've gone, won't you? I'll allow you to shut the shop for half-an-hour. No more, mind.'

'Is he never going to stop these ridiculous pilgrimages?' Edwin said. 'I imagine that's where you're going?'

'Where else? You know Juby.'

His shoulders slumped and, glancing at Midge from beneath exaggeratedly defeated brows, he shuffled out as Poor Little Browbeaten Man. For once there was nothing amusing in his performance.

When she next saw him, about half an hour later, she was at the kitchen table wrapping the sandwiches Inger had started and left her to finish. He came rattling down the back stairs into the kitchen. 'How ya doin', kid?' enquired a hoodlum from an old film noir, reaching for the bread knife and the remaining third of the loaf.

'OK.'

He sawed off a doorstep, lathered it with butter, and was about to sink his teeth into it when a black shape filled the entrance to the corridor between the kitchen and the shop. Juby Bench had returned ten minutes ago and been with Inger ever since, in the office.

'Ed,' Juby said in sombre greeting.

Edwin set his snack aside untasted, wiped buttery fingers on the seams of his trousers.

'Here again then, Jube.'

Juby clumped down the two stone steps into the kitchen. The lower floor allowed him to raise his head, but even here the ceiling flattened his grey mane. Brittle flakes of dry old paint spattered the shoulders of his black jacket like dandruff.

'Here again, boy. Keeping well?'

'Mustn't grumble,' Edwin said. 'Yourself?'

'Could grumble, no point.'

After which they seemed to have nothing to say to one another. Silence fell like a ton of cottonwool bricks as the two men, absolute physical opposites – the one unnaturally lanky with Strewelpeter hair, the other short, pot-bellied and bald – virtually froze, avoiding eye-contact. Midge was grateful when Inger breezed in blowing dust off the cane picnic hamper she'd just emptied of old receipts and invoices.

'All done?' she asked Midge.

While they packed the hamper, Edwin and Juby remained where they were, as if turned to wax. Inger, obviously used to such behaviour when these two were together, did not remark on this. Only when everything was ready, the hamper closed, did she demand action.

'Come along, you two,' she said briskly to Midge and Juby, 'or we'll be lunching at four. Edwin: sell books. That is your sole purpose in life today.'

'How am I supposed to mind the shop *and* cook for tonight?' Edwin said.

'Just mind the shop. I never liked fish pie anyway.'

'You didn't? You don't? You've never said. All these years.'

'I didn't want to hurt your feelings.'

Inger touched her lips with her fingertips, then his

26

forehead, as though dispensing a blessing. He did not react, but as Midge followed the others out, she glanced at him to nod farewell. He was staring at the door Inger and Juby had left by, on his face an expression of cold fury.

Four

Having been parked in the sweltering sun all morning, Inger's eight-year-old-blue Volvo was like an oven inside. Juby Bench asked Midge if she would like to sit in the front, but Inger wouldn't hear of it – 'She'll be fine in the back, won't you Midge?' – so he took the passenger seat while Midge, seething quietly, clipped herself into the seat behind him. Before moving off, Inger plucked her sunglasses from the folding visor over the windscreen. The silver frames, plunging into the thick dark hair over her ears, emphasised the hank of white that sprang from her crown. Midge sifted through her shoulder bag for her own glasses. They weren't there, and now they were off and it was too late to go back for them. Knowing she hadn't got her shades, the light became all the brighter. Painfully so.

Last night Inger had taken the precaution of draping a towel over the steering wheel, but it was still too hot to grip, so her fingers danced on the wheel for the first half-mile or so, as she chattered constantly, loudly, exhilaratedly. Juby's conversation was more measured, but Midge, feeling about four years old strapped in the back, scowled at his long neck, creased as an old map. He was an intruder. She didn't want him there. Didn't want any of them.

Once out of Steepridge the road dipped and wound through hills and hollows divided by drystone walls and fields of various shades and hues. Blinded by the dazzling white escarpment of a chalk quarry, Midge hunched low in her seat for most of the journey, arms folded, sighing with determined boredom at all the scattered farmsteads, the steeples of churches, the brown thatch of cottages, isolated clumps of woodland on horizons, until, between hills, she glimpsed the sea. This brought her to immediate attention, straining for a better view. She'd forgotten how close Steepridge was to the coast. In all the years of brief 'duty visits' down this way, no one had ever taken her there. Well, perhaps today they would. This place they were going to (some village Juby and Edwin had lived in as boys), maybe it was on the coast. If so, the day might not be quite such a washout after all.

When, without warning, Inger span the wheel and the Volvo jerked onto a descending side road, Midge was the only one who was not prepared. She gave a little shriek while reaching in several directions at once for something to hold on to. By the time she'd grabbed the seat in front they were the other side of a short tunnel of trees, and flying between unploughed fields defined by barbed-wire fences and gates that bore enamel signs showing a silhouetted walking man, and the words:

MILITARY FIRING RANGE
KEEP OUT

The first of these signs brought a sharp retort from Juby Bench, two words, growled fiercely, which sent Midge's eyes flying to the mirror, to meet Inger's. She diverted her gaze to the windscreen. Barren fields, barbed-wire, warning signs, none of it mattered, for directly ahead sat a cone of brilliant blue, shimmering between ochre cliffs. She leant forward as the road rose and fell, twisted and turned, yet always delivered them back to this excellent course. They never seemed to get much closer, but it couldn't be far now. Minutes, surely, and she'd be strutting along the beach with sand between her toes, or kicking pebbles, inspecting shells.

'Here we are!' Inger cried suddenly.

Midge craned her neck. They were approaching a low stone wall behind which stood the ground floors and walls of a linked row of ruined cottages. The sea had disappeared, and for a moment it looked as if the road, along with the car, would end at the wall, but both veered sharply to the left and carried them past a small pond and a group of trees, up an incline to an open plain of stony ground. There, Inger found a place well away from a number of other parked cars, jerked hers to a halt, and switched the engine off with a flourish. At once, with the urgency of someone keen to vomit, Juby Bench threw his door open and leapt out. Inger got out at a more dignified pace, while Midge remained in her seat, fed up all over again. So much for the sea.

'Coming, Midge, or staying there all day?'

She unclipped her belt and got out, hoping her displeasure showed. The sun smacked the top of her head like a reprimand. After the breeze through the open windows the heat was unbelievable. She screwed her eyes up against the light. They were in a wide valley encircled by green hills. Nothing much to see, though Juby seemed to have found something to look at. He stood, gazing down the slope towards the ruins they'd passed. Midge heard the boot lid bounce and Inger hauling the hamper out. She made a duty-move to help, but her grandmother, no malingerer, tossed a tartan blanket onto the car roof, jammed a straw hat with a crimson bandana on her head, and slammed the boot.

'Spot of shade, I think. Down there?'

She indicated the grove of trees between the car park and the ruins. Midge shrugged. Wherever. All the same to her.

'Juby?'

At the sound of his name Juby Bench set off down the slope like one who'd been kicked sharply from behind. In spite of the heat he still wore his enormous black jacket, which, unbuttoned, flapped about him like badly-coordinated wings.

'You could always carry this as you're going that way!' Inger bawled after him. She might as well not have spoken, for he kept going without any kind of acknowledgement. 'Just us then,' she said to Midge. 'Bring the blanket, will you.'

'What about the windows?' Midge asked, hauling the blanket off the roof as Inger headed for the trees with the hamper.

'Windows?'

'They're still open.'

'Leave them. Be hot as Hades in there when we get back, even as they are.'

Midge set off after her, the hot, hairy blanket rough against her bare arms. When they reached the trees and shade, they spread the blanket across the flattest section of grass they could find. There was no sign of Juby.

'Where's he gone?' Midge asked.

Inger dropped to her knees and threw back the lid of the hamper. 'Oh, he'll be wanting to see what they've been up to since last year.'

'What who's been up to?'

'Who? Why, the – tuh!' She broke off. A bee had landed on the sandwiches and seemed keen to get inside the silver foil. 'Oh no you don't, you little...'

She found a stick and tried to coax the bee away without hurting it. When it transferred its attentions to the stick, she tossed it away, the bee still clinging to it. Seconds later, a Scottish terrier bounded from behind a nearby tree, seized the stick in its jaws, and ran round in several joyous circles before dropping it with a yelp and scampering back the way it had come, off sticks for life.

Asked if she would prefer a tuna or cheese sandwich, Midge took the cheese and a bag of crisps.

'D'you like picnics?' Inger asked as they settled down to eat.

'Can't remember the last one,' she replied round a mouthful.

The last one. She must have been half her present height. Mum and Dad weren't big on days out. You couldn't sort the world out on a picnic. But here she was, suddenly, unexpectedly, picnicking after all these years, and, sea or no sea, it felt rather pleasant in the shade of these laden boughs. Inger sat a few feet away, supporting herself with the heel of one hand as she nibbled round the crusts of the sandwich in the other. It was quite a thing to see this restless woman so relaxed, but as she didn't know her well enough to feel comfortable with her silence, Midge grabbed the first subject that came to mind.

'Those signs we passed on the way. All the barbed-wire and stuff...'

'MoD,' said Inger, still nibbling.

'Sorry?'

'Ministry of Defence. This is a military zone. Army training and weapons testing ground.'

Midge peered out from their shady enclosure. What was she on about? Private cars came and went as they pleased, families strolled with cameras, kids ran all over the place, squealing. She could see the roof of a small church amid the trees beyond the ruined cottages, and a great many more trees all around, with bits of other buildings showing here and there, while to her right, on the hillside, cows grazed undisturbed. Military zone? Army training ground? Weapons?

Her puzzlement had been observed. 'This is the Rouklye Valley,' Inger said, as if that explained everything. It did not. She saw this as well. 'I was forgetting. Another time, as far as you're concerned. Before my time too, really. Well, never mind, ancient history, let's just enjoy our day.'

She leant forward to pour tea from the flask into one of the three plastic cups they'd brought, handed it to Midge, then poured one for herself and set it in a hollow she created for it in the blanket. She had barely done this when a large multi-coloured ball careered down the slope from the car park, glanced off a tree, and sent the cup flying. Midge expected her to leap to her feet, as her mother would certainly have done, and dab furiously at the wet patch on the blanket while glaring at the small boy who ran to retrieve the ball. But Inger Bjølstad and her daughter were two very different kettles of fish. All Inger did was change the angle of her hat, sigh as the boy scuttled back to his parents with his ball, and pat the spilt tea with a couple of the paper napkins.

They'd just about settled down again when Juby Bench emerged from a wooded area some way below them and to their left. Midge did not welcome his return, but the look of him took her by surprise. The upright determined figure that had stalked away now appeared very downcast, arms hanging limply at his sides as he stumbled up the uneven slope. He said nothing as he seated himself on a corner of the blanket and crossed his legs at the ankle. His feet, bare in open-toed sandals that, like him, had seen better days, were enormous, with long jagged toenails.

'Is it much changed since last year?' Inger asked him.

Juby stared blankly at her, seemingly defeated by the question, and turned away, started tearing the grass around his feet. Midge, glancing his way a minute later, saw him stop what he was doing, frown at his hands as though catching them in some antisocial act, and gently gather up the torn blades of grass and place them, very precisely, side by side as if hoping they would grow again if treated with care.

He perked up a bit when he finally got to work on the sandwiches, which he gobbled, and the tea, which he slurped. He seemed much more at ease by the time he started on the apple Inger cut into pieces for him with a small pearl-handled knife she carried in a suede sheath for such purposes. He still didn't have much to say, but Midge began to get used to his being there. She could put up with him as long as she didn't have to talk to him.

Then Inger spoiled everything.

'Midge hasn't been here before, Jube. Why don't you give her the guided tour?'

Her heart plummeted as the tousled head and the great beak of a nose turned, and those sharp pale eyes settled on her.

'She might not want a guided tour,' he growled.

'Midge?' Inger said.

The prospect of being shown round a crummy old village by this peculiar man didn't thrill her at all, but she wasn't good at saying no, so...

'Don't mind.'

He was on his feet in a trice, so eager to get going that Midge was forced to cram the last of her crisps in her mouth and also rise.

'You?' Juby asked Inger.

'I've seen it.'

She fell onto her elbows, then to her back, and tugged her hat over her eyes, dismissing the pair of them. Juby took his jacket off and dropped it on the grass, then loped away rolling up the sleeves of his off-white shirt.

'Gra-an,' Midge hissed.

Inger raised the brim of the hat. 'Yes, my darling?'

The look in her shaded eyes suggested that she knew very well how uncomfortable Midge was about this, and found it amusing.

'Oh, *forget* it.'

Never before had she spoken that way to her grandmother, but she was too angry to care if she caused offence. She swung about and headed after Juby Bench wondering what the hell you talk about to an old weirdo like him.

FIVE

Juby stopped at the pond they'd passed on the way to the car park. On the far side of it, a man in a T-shirt emblazoned with the words SUNSHINE STATE leaned over to take photographs of bulrushes. There were no bulrushes on Juby's side, but there were reeds and water lilies, which he stood gazing down at. He was speaking even before Midge caught up with him.

'...a bit since I was a lad. Nothing to take snaps of then, the way that fella's doing. It was a working pond. Watering hole where the cattle stopped off for a drink on the way to milking. Horses too.'

'Oh, you milked horses then, did you?' she muttered to herself.

'It wasn't clean like this. Nothing like this clean. There

was masses of spawn on the surface, and we'd dip our hands in and pull it around, have races with it along the banks, dragging it.' He chuckled at the memory, a dry-as-dust, older-than-God chuckle. 'Made your own amusement in those days. No telly then.'

No telly now, she thought, eying the spawn-free water with distaste.

'And eels,' Juby said.

'What?'

'Thick with 'em, it was. Only little ones, but slippery old boys, not easy to catch. You had to trick them.' He glanced at her, apparently assuming that she was interested. 'What we did was, we bound up hazel twigs and sank them in the water for a day or so, then we'd hoik 'em out, quick as winking, and those bundles'd be full to bursting. Good bait, eel. The mackerel could never resist a bit of nice fresh eel. Some always found their way into the pot, though. Eels are very tasty, done right.'

So saying, he stalked away, following the curve of the landscaped pond, towards the stone wall that skirted the row of ruined cottages. This time Midge dallied, but it was an unnoticed rebellion, and short-lived. She didn't know the man, had no idea how his temper worked. Some way ahead of her yet, he reached the wall and peered over it at an antiquated telephone kiosk, a cream-and-red affair topped with a spike like the business end of a spear. Beyond the wall, visitors ambled in and out of the ruins, touching the old stones and taking pictures as if at the Parthenon or the Coliseum or something. One couple in particular caught Midge's eye as she drew near: a distinctly overweight woman in tight white leggings that bulged in all the wrong places, and her much thinner husband or boyfriend in shorts and a pink shirt that clashed horribly with his ginger hair. The man must have announced that he wanted to take his beloved's picture, because she positioned herself in the doorless doorway of one of the cottages, one knee raised, the sole of her shoe against the stone, a podgy hand behind her head like an old-time pin-up. 'Say Caerphilly,' the photographer said, and his model giggled, and he took the picture.

As Midge joined Juby, he indicated the kiosk on the other side of the wall, and said: 'I did that.'

She looked. There was a 'Closed' sign on the glass-panelled door. Through the glass she saw an old black phone with A and B buttons.

'Did what?'

Reaching over, Juby traced a crack in one of the panels. 'This. When I was fifteen. Threw half a brick at it.'

'Why did you do that?'

'Why? I was fifteen.'

Well, so am I, she thought, but I don't go round smashing windows. She kept this to herself.

He was about to lead the way through a gap in the wall where a small gate must once have been, when the overweight young woman who fancied herself as a glamour girl launched herself towards it, followed by her partner. Juby stood aside to let them through. They gave no sign of noticing either him or his small courtesy, or even his 'Pleasure,' to their ill-matched backs.

There were four adjoining cottages within the wall. A fifth building, also joined but much smaller, was the only one with a door and a roof. The roof was formed of crudely-cut grey slate, and on the door, which was padlocked, a notice asked visitors not to pick the wild flowers, which amused Midge because there were no flowers in the vicinity, wild or tame.

Juby had gone straight to the second cottage along, where he stooped to look in the doorway. 'This was the post office and village shop,' he informed her.

'Oh yes?' she said, already bored.

He ducked inside. She followed with a long-suffering sigh, and found a crumbling interior open to the skies, ivy reaching across exposed walls to which ragged portions of ancient plaster clung. An iron fire-grate teetered on a ledge where a ceiling and upper floor had once been, while beneath their feet ailing weeds struggled between uneven grey paving slabs, and fragile year-old leaves crunched underfoot. The place smelt of nettles and moss, the dust of an overheated summer, and had nothing whatever to commend it.

'Looks bigger empty,' said Juby Bench. 'When the counter was in, shelves stocked, customer or two chatting, it was a right jam in here.'

Sunlight entered the broken building in tall bright spirals, picking out hovering dust motes. Watching the dust's leisurely dance, Midge's mind wandered. Her thoughts were still adrift when the whispers started. Whispers so indistinct that they registered only gradually; but once her attention was caught she glanced about for whoever it was that had followed them in. There was no one else, just the two of them. The whispers faded.

'—get anything here,' Juby was saying. 'The women bought their wool here, their needles and thread, cleaning materials, candles, matches. Men bought their baccy and bootlaces. There were sweets behind the counter in big glass jars, sides of bacon on hooks, cheese and butter in slabs to be sliced up as you pleased. You don't get shops like that today.'

No, Midge thought, shrugging off the whispers and the shivers they had induced, you get supermarkets, and a good job too.

She retreated to the doorway, waited there, hoping he would notice that he was talking to himself and take the hint. He didn't. He was facing the other way, still reminiscing.

'—so many parcels and packages on the counter you could barely see the postmistress. Mrs Ritter, her name was. Little lady, but tough, tough as a kipper. The lads used to see what they could get away with. If she was in a good mood she might give them a quarter of boiled sweets or some liquorice, but she wasn't—'

Midge switched off. If he was going to give a detailed account of who once did what in every building in the village, even the ruined ones, she'd end up screaming, she knew she would. She heard him chuckle at another memory, groaned as the post came on a cart from Wareham and the postman passed the day before the afternoon collection on his allotment, or fishing. Well, let him fish.

She stepped outside and watched people stroll by in small groups, pairs, singly. The singles passed by in worlds of their own. Lucky them, she thought, setting her back against the wall. Behind her, the old man's voice continued to rumble along like the postman's cart. Closing her eyes against the day, the light, the people, her mind drifted once again, and almost at once she might have been anywhere, any other place or time, where parents stayed home, people took notice of her, and she was beautiful. The daydream was shattered by the sound of giant feet crushing brittle leaves in the shell of a building she leant against. Juby was on his way out. Rather than fall in with him again so soon, she darted away, weaving around and between camera-toting strollers.

At the end of the row, a short path through a shady dell delivered her to a dirt roadway that swung between the last cottage and the elevated churchyard opposite. A little way along, to her left, stood a small gabled building with a recently-tiled roof and red-painted window frames, but some distance beyond this, amid trees, she spotted a collapsed house, then another, and then half a wall of one more. What's with all the ruins? she wondered, while telling herself that it was nothing to her.

She crossed the road to the churchyard steps, but did not climb them, choosing instead to stand nearby, in the shade of an old oak. A large stone set in the ground before the oak informed her that it had been planted in 1911 to mark the coronation of George V. Fascinating, she thought, unfascinated. From the tree she could see along the entire row of cottages, and Juby emerging from the third of them. Must be looking for her, she decided. Wondering where I've got to. She watched him go into the last cottage. He remained inside for two or three minutes before coming out and entering the grove through which she had preceded him. Seconds later, without any sign that he was seeking her, he was loping across the road towards her, mopping his brow with a handkerchief the size of a tea-towel. He must have spotted her back there then; known where she'd gone all along.

'What's up?' he asked as he reached the shade of the oak.

'Up?'

'You look puzzled.'

'I was just wondering where the village is,' she replied, unsure that she'd been wondering anything of the sort.

'You're in it,' he informed her.

'No, I mean the proper village, the part that's not ruined.'

'It's all ruined.'

'Eh?'

'Except that church and the schoolhouse over there. They've tarted those up for show, like the pond.' He stuffed the handkerchief back in his pocket; set a shoulder against the trunk of the tree. 'Place's been deserted since the war. I thought everyone knew that.'

'The war? Which war?'

He looked at her as if she were an imbecile. 'Which war do you think: the Boer War, the Hundred Years War, the Wars of the Roses?' His tone was sharp, blue eyes cold. 'I was a boy here, how old d'you think I am?'

'Well, the...there are always wars,' she stammered. 'It's hard to keep up sometimes.'

Juby Bench slipped his hands in his trouser pockets, turned his loose change around; nodded to himself. The girl had a point.

'The last *world* war,' he said finally.

'Oh. So, was it...' – she hardly liked to ask in case he snapped again – '...bombed or something?'

He didn't snap. He said, almost with a chuckle: 'Bombed!', and raked the sky beyond the tree's reach as though expecting the Luftwaffe any minute. Then he looked at her again, less forbiddingly this time. 'Didn't your gran tell you they turfed us out?'

'Turfed you out?'

'Churchill's government. December 1943, just before Christmas. Cleared the entire valley, right down to the coast. Evicted over two hundred-and-twenty people from a hundred or more properties, including eleven smallholdings, five farms. Said they needed the land to test weapons, train troops. They also said we could

47

come back when it was all over. Didn't happen. Bet that isn't in your school history books.'

'What do you mean, it didn't happen?' Midge said.

'By the war's end the Army's feet were too far under the table. Didn't want to give it up, and they didn't – ever. Everything you see, and a whole lot more that you don't, is still theirs to this day.'

'But all these people...' She waved a hand to indicate the visitors wandering wherever they wished, sitting on walls, taking pictures, kids squealing off in all directions.

'It's August,' said Juby Bench.

'So?'

'The one month of the year the little soldier boys and girls climb back in their boxes and the public's allowed in.' He snorted. 'The public! Day-trippers picking through our old houses in their nice summer clothes, taking home picture postcards from the church of what it used to be like. They have no idea, girl. No bloody idea.'

He pushed himself away from the tree and ambled along the road to the building with the red window frames. Midge followed, looking around her with just a little more interest than before.

SIX

The schoolhouse door opened into a narrow cloakroom with coat pegs on either side. Each peg had a small card by it with the name of a pupil who had once attended the school. Her eye was caught by one of the names: Violent Croke. She gaped. *Violent Croke?!* Closer inspection, however, revealed that there was no 'n'.

She read the rest of the names without adding letters: Dorothy Ferris, Walter Richards, Kathleen Richards, Henry Braine, John Bellman, Vera Bellman, Tommy Ochart, Elizabeth Fannon, John Miller, Lizzie Naylor, Fred Day, and a number of others. Above the pegs on one wall hung a framed photograph, cracked and brown with age, showing the children, aged from about five to fourteen, to whom the pegs had belonged during their years of attendance. A youngish schoolmistress, unsmiling, stood to one side of them, hands folded neatly in front of her. Midge counted twenty-two pegs and twenty-two names, but thirty-one children in the picture. This suggested that there were either more pegs originally or that nine of the kids in the photo did without or doubled up. In the middle of the front row young Billy Brooker, who looked as if he'd just been told to sit up straight and didn't want to, held a small writing slate on which the teacher had chalked 'Rouklye School 1912'. A typed note beside the photo stated that this same Billy Brooker was later drowned, at the age of seventeen, in a boating accident in Crowbarrow Bay.

The school itself was a single, heavily-beamed, chapel-like room. A pair of oil lamps dangled on long chains from the whitewashed ceiling. There was a brick fireplace with an old wood stove, and a series of linked desks with fixed benches. Samples of the work of former pupils were laid out on the desks, under glass like museum exhibits.

'Is any of this yours?' Midge asked Juby as he drifted away from her like a quietly-freed shadow.

He glanced at the work and shook his head. 'Long before my day. I didn't go to school here anyway.'

A large blackboard stood on a sturdy easel to one side

of the fireplace. The board's main headings were painted on. The rest, changed daily during the 'public month', were neatly hand-written in chalk.

Welcome
to
Rouklye School
15th August

Weather Outlook
Sunny, hot, cooling sea breeze

Max temp 29c

Look out for
*Adders basking in the sun
Weasels around village*

Juby stepped up onto the platform at the far end of the room, squeezed himself onto the bench fixed to one side of the broader-than-usual desk that stood there, and stuck his chin on a fist to gaze out of the big bright end window. He's an odd one, Midge thought. The way he looks, behaves. Even his name was odd. 'Juby

Bench' was certainly on a par with 'Violet Croke', even without the 'n'.

A small giggle behind her. She turned to see who had come in. No one. For the second time in less than twenty minutes her spine tingled, but when she saw a young family passing beyond the window she decided that one of the children must have briefly popped its head in. To pass the time until Juby deigned to lead the way out, she strolled along the desks examining the work under glass. There were crayon and pencil drawings, childish poems about nature, the weather, home life. There were also sums, spelling tests, things about religion, and 'lines'. The work didn't seem all that old-fashioned, and she found it hard to imagine that the kids who'd produced it would be very old now – those who were still about at all. Most would be long dead, like Billy Brooker. It wasn't so easy to be amused by their school work, or their names, when you remembered that.

She extended her fingers to the unlit fire, imagining the warmth of a good blaze on a freezing winter's day, then moved along to the piano, an old upright. Tempted to sit down and plink-plank-plunk a bit, a glance at Juby, preoccupied by the window, dissuaded her. Instead, she went to a display case that offered a selection of hand-written entries from the school register, which seemed to have doubled as a diary.

July 13th, 1911   *Not so good an attendance this week. Children are kept away while mothers carry food to the hayfield.*

May 24th, 1912   *Ernest Mawer has been away all week with a swollen face. Irene Day has been away since Wednesday owing to sickness.*

Aug. 2nd, 1912   *Irene Day leaves today being 14 years of age next week. I am rather sorry to lose my older children.*

Oct. 26th, 1913   *The attendance is again lowered by the absence of Tommy Ochart who has not been to school since the holiday owing to having no boots.*

'Show you my house if you like.'

She looked towards the platform. Juby's hulking silhouette at the desk.

'Your houssss...?'

The word skidded to a halt. There were two silhouettes at the desk, the second sitting across from Juby: a boy, thin and rangy, no less wild-haired than the man. She tried to speak, but her tongue refused to let go the roof of her mouth.

A sudden cacophony behind her caused her to spin round as half-a-dozen children burst in, followed by a quartet of adults. The adults clustered in the doorway, peering about without quite entering, while their less inhibited progeny threw themselves on the desks, laughing, squealing, shouting – 'Miss! Miss! Please, Miss!' – and sticking their hands in the air to attract an invisible teacher's attention.

An angry growl from the far end. Midge turned to see Juby jump to his feet. The other figure – the boy – was gone. Juby charged through the room, head down like a bull intent on getting out of the china shop come what may. She stepped smartly aside, as did the people crowding the doorway, and followed him at a more temperate pace, mumbling apologies to the parents.

The light outside was so blinding that she couldn't see him at first, but when she managed to make him out she forgot to breathe for several seconds. He stood against the churchyard wall opposite, in the shade of an elderly horse-chestnut, the sun, pouring through a break in the foliage, picking him out and bleaching him away almost to nothing.*

As she approached, Juby stepped out from the tree and led the way down a steep, narrow path to the building he wanted to show her, from the top of which she could see far more of the house than she would be able to at the bottom. Unlike the cottages and most of the other buildings he would point out before he was done, this one still had much of its upper storey, though its roof had long since caved in. A mass of trees crowded in on it, along with a cordon of high, dense weeds that tangled around barbed-wire and metal signs warning visitors to proceed no further for their own safety.

Upon descending the path, all she could see of the house was the top portion of two upper windows and the crest of a gable end. Juby, being so tall, was not similarly disadvantaged. Expecting him to launch into an interminable monologue about his wonderful childhood here, she was not disappointed when he said nothing at all; merely stood a while, gazing at the house, then turned away to continue the tour.

---

* That evening she described this scene in the first of several proposed letters to Nessa Friedman, intending to mail them just before Ness returned from holiday. She made no mention of the boy sitting across from Juby in the schoolroom – an illusion too ludicrous for words, even to her best friend.

SEVEN

Inger and Edwin's house was seventeenth century, but not nearly as attractive or interesting as those two words make it sound. At least a century and a half past its best, it was all rather wonky, both inside and out, with sagging ceilings, banging pipes that regularly froze in winter, and tiles that popped off the roof when starlings landed. The bookshop took up most of the ground floor, though the stone-flagged kitchen was a fair size, and, off the short corridor between the two, there was the former pantry that served as Inger's office. When there were browsers in the shop, she would retreat to this cubbyhole so as not to put them off, but a hatch between the two allowed her to respond quickly to enquiries or calls for service – and to keep an eye out for shoplifters.

There was no one in the shop, customer or thief, when Midge brought her a cup of coffee and a couple of digestives the morning after the trip to Rouklye, but Inger was in the office anyway, 'cooking the books,' she said. Then she said something else.

'Midge, a friend has invited you to visit her children this afternoon. I've said you'll go, hope it's all right. If nothing else, a visit to them will give you something to be grateful for.'

'Grateful for?'

'That you don't live there.'

And just like that it was agreed, without her agreeing to anything at all.

The Barstows lived some minutes' walk away, just outside the village and up a bit of hill. Edwin was assigned the task of escorting her there. For this, he donned the shapeless cricket hat that he'd never played cricket in. 'Cruel woman,' he said as they started out.

'Who?' Midge asked.

'The Valkyrie. I wouldn't have inflicted the Brat on you.'

'The Brat?'

'The second Barstow male. Every time I have the misfortune to be within reach of him, my hands twitch with longing to encircle his scrawny little neck. What did you make of Rouklye?'

Her step faltered. This was the first time he'd mentioned yesterday's excursion, though they'd exchanged several words since.

'It was…different,' she conceded.

'Your gran says Juby gave you the Tour. Can't have taken long if he just showed you the village. What did he have to say about the place?'

'Well, he told me about everyone having to clear out during the war.' She would have been happy to leave it at that, but he seemed to want more; so, rather lamely, she added: 'Showed me a pane of glass he broke in the phone box when he was fifteen...'

'Did he now? Well, that says a lot.'

'What do you mean?'

He glanced about like one who believes the trees might be wired.

'In the mid-eighties Rouklye was used for a film about the Tolpuddle Martyrs – heard of them?'

'Not sure.'

'Bunch of nineteenth century Dorset labourers who agitated for a living wage and got sentenced to transportation and penal servitude for their pains. Rouklye was the only village in the county the film people could find that wasn't spoilt by time. Ruined, yes, but not spoilt, on account of its not having been lived in for forty years. By the time they'd done their stuff the place looked a treat. Authentic-looking false fronts on the cottages, thatched roofs, a square tower on the church. I was an extra.'

'An extra? A film extra? You?'

'Disgruntled villager in a smock. Felt a right berk, I can tell you. Fortunately, they left me on the cutting room floor. But the telephone box. There was a storm one night, terrible gale in off the sea, and some of the film-makers' scaffolding came down on it. Virtual write-off, but they restored it, repainted it, put new glass in. So whoever cracked that pane it wasn't Juby Bench.'

'Maybe he doesn't know about the storm,' she said.

'Maybe a lot of things.' A little further on, his voice dropped to a whisper. 'Midge. Word to the wise. If the man of the house is at home, don't mention Rouklye. His granddad helped supervise the '43 evacuation and Wystan gets a mite prickly if he hears anything against the takeover. Guilty family conscience, I reckon, but don't quote me. Get ready to duck the missiles now.'

He stopped before a moderately imposing Georgian house, and, of course, Midge stopped with him. As they did so, a woman in her early forties rose out of a large shrub just inside the driveway.

'Ah. Our visitors.'

'Just one,' Edwin said. 'I'm not stopping. Wild horses wouldn't make me, so don't try and persuade me. Midge, Mrs Barstow.'

She was short and pleasantly plump, with a lively face, ash blonde hair curling around a lime-green headscarf. She dropped her pinking shears, removed one of her gardening gloves, extended the hand it had contained.

'Jilly. Pleased to meet you, Midge. I've heard so much about you.'

'She's heard nothing,' Edwin said out of the side of his mouth.

'Nat and Henry are looking forward to meeting you too,' Jilly said. 'Between ourselves, I think the holidays are dragging a bit. You'll be a nice distraction for them.'

Great, she thought. I'm not a person, I'm a distraction. And two boys. It got worse by the minute.

The lady stepped back, drawing her by the hand she was still holding. 'You can go now,' she said to Edwin.

He looked grateful for the dismissal. 'Luck, Midge,' he said, and, as Humphrey Bogart: 'Gonna need it, kid.' Switching to Charlie Chaplin, he headed for home whirling an invisible cane, one foot on the curb, one in the gutter.

To Midge's relief it turned out that Henry was short for Henrietta. She was eight, and petite and sweet where her older brother, at fourteen – though he looked and behaved two years younger – was neither. Nathaniel Barstow was extremely thin, pallid of complexion, with fair hair that flopped over one eye, and a lip that curled when his mother introduced him to Midge.

'Nat, why don't you show Midge your room?'

The eye not concealed by hair narrowed suspiciously. 'Whaffor?'

'Because she'd like to see it – wouldn't you, Midge?'

No, Midge thought, but made a passionless 'mmm' sound.

'Don't want to,' said Nat the Brat sulkily.

'Come on now, darling. Midge is our guest.'

'Not mine, she isn't.' And he turned and stomped upstairs.

'He's shy,' Jilly said with slightly strained brightness. 'He's very proud of his room, loves to show it off. You go after him, Midge, while I squeeze us some lemon squash.'

Midge glanced at Henrietta, kneeling on the floor weaving model cars in and out of an obstacle course of tins and cereal packets. Henry caught her glance. 'You can play with me,' she offered.

'I'd rather,' she whispered, but the choice wasn't hers to make. She went upstairs. On the square landing at the top she was faced with several closed doors. 'Hello?'

When there was no reply she knocked on the nearest one. Again no response, so she rapped lightly on each of the others in turn, wishing she could go back down. Even toy cars and cereal boxes with an eight year old would have the edge on this. It was the last door that turned out to front the room she was obliged to seek, identified by a wordless shout that was anything but welcoming. She bridled – who did the little creep think he was? – and spun round, headed for the stairs.

A second before she started down, however, Nathaniel's door flew back and he stood in the doorway. She did a double-take. His jeans and T-shirt had been replaced by camouflage trousers and jacket.

'Thought you wanted to see my room,' he said.

'Whatever gave you that idea?'

'Can if you want.'

He stood to attention, holding the door open for her. She hesitated, but returned, walked past him into his room – and reared back in amazement.

The walls of Nathaniel Barstow's room were covered with posters, prints and photographs depicting air battles, land battles, sea battles, in which guns blazed, bombs exploded, and depth charges sped towards underwater targets. There were infantrymen with fixed bayonets belting hell-for-leather across deformed landscapes; men sprawling on smoke-shrouded battlefields; soldiers leaping from trenches, torn apart by mortar shells. But the pictures were only the half of it. Every space and surface was crammed with small replicas of machines of war, and there was a battle game on the floor with armies ranged against one another. Even the duvet depicted a scene of conflict. There were guns of various kinds too, and hand-grenades. The guns didn't look quite real, but the grenades did.

On the wall behind the bed, an enormous map of the world was covered with curved red arrows suggesting points of attack or troop movement, along with a multitude of coloured pins. One of the pins was situated very near where she thought her parents were right now. To think, they were all the way out there in the South Pacific trying to stop some military dictatorship testing weapons that could kill thousands – millions perhaps – and here was she, their only child, being given a private view of this little twit's war room.

'Bet you never saw a room like this before,' Nathaniel said proudly.

'Not in this lifetime,' she replied.

'I'm gonna join the Army when I'm old enough.'

'Really.'

'My dad says I can start training to be an officer as soon as I leave school. I'm gonna be a gen—'

The crunch of wheels on gravel cut him short. Nathaniel leapt onto the window seat and leant out. 'Dad!' he yelled. 'Dad!'

Midge also looked out. A man in the uniform of an Army officer was getting out of a gleaming black Saab. He looked up and waved. Nat the Brat's role model was home.

Major Wystan Barstow unbuttoned his collar and tugged his tie loose as he strolled through the house, stepped over Henry and her cars, and out onto the patio.

'This heat!'

He slipped his jacket off, slung it over one of the green garden chairs, and sank gratefully into the lounger his wife had been using earlier to enhance her already glowing tan.

'Lemon squash, darling?'

'Lemon squash? You have to be joking.'

Jilly went inside and Wystan closed his eyes, let his jaw go slack. Peace. Until the rifle barrel plunged into his mouth.

'You're dead meat,' growled his son and heir.

Barstow senior's eyes flew open. 'Unnggh?'

The young soldier standing over him, finger on trigger,

leered triumphantly, but his father wasn't an officer for nothing. Deftly removing the barrel from his mouth, he rolled off the lounger and wrestled the boy to the ground.

Obliged to shadow him until she received new orders, Midge had followed Nathaniel out. She winced at his thin voice, his bellows and threats as he fought his father, longing to be anywhere but here.

'Wystan, this is Midge. Inger and Edwin's granddaughter.'

Major Barstow froze. He looked up, disconcerted to find a stranger watching him wrestling with his son on the ground. Nat continued to flail, but his father said something to him which, after repeating it more sharply, caused him to lie still.

Wystan got to his feet and pulled the knot of his tie from under his left ear, a lopsided grin forming beneath his dark moustache. He proffered Midge his hand.

'Hi. Visiting with the oldies then, are you?'

'For a few weeks,' Jilly answered for her. 'While her parents are away on...business.'

The last word was so loaded that her husband couldn't fail to miss it. Then he recalled the many reports of the campaigning Millers and their crackpot organisation's mission to save the world from itself. He withdrew his hand, which Jilly put a can of cold beer into. He punctured the can, gulped at it, and kept on gulping as though it were his first drink for days.

'Midge?'

The promised lemon squash, in a tall slim tumbler. 'Thanks.' She took it and sipped. It was good. So good that she drained half the glass before she could bear to lower it, understanding very well how the officer of the house felt about his cold beer.

'Dad! Let's fight some more!'

'Not now, Nat, too hot. And we have a visitor.'

Nathaniel was not pleased. 'I want to *fight*!' he snarled.

'Yeah, well I don't, all right? Now don't have one of your fits. Go and cool off in the fish pond or something.'

Nathaniel's eyes were furious slits as his father sank back onto the lounger. Midge glanced at Henry, who'd come out when her brother started playing up. Young as she was, Henry knew him all too well. Knew that he wasn't one to stroll off quietly when told. She watched him turn about and stalk down the garden. The garden being long and well-stocked, he was soon lost from sight. Henry touched Midge's arm.

'Show you my room now?'

'Midge might not want to, dear.' Jilly plucked her husband's jacket from the chair and folded it neatly over her arm, smoothing creases with the flat of her hand.

'Oh, I don't mind,' Midge said.

Henry gripped her wrist and tugged her towards the house, but a sharp yell from down the garden skidded her to a halt.

'Nat?' said Jilly in alarm.

She dropped Wystan's jacket and hurried down the path to rescue her son from whatever hideous fate threatened him. Wystan closed his eyes. 'That boy,' he muttered, but when another distant cry reached him he sighed, eased himself out of the lounger, and went wearily after his wife.

'Natty playing silly buggers,' Henry said to Midge, but she waited out of curiosity, which forced Midge to wait with her.

When the trio returned, Wystan was furious, Jilly was upset, and Nathaniel, grumbling incoherently, was drenched from head to foot.

'Sometimes, boy,' his father was saying, 'I have serious doubts about your sanity. When I say cool off in the fish pond I'm joking, right? You know what a joke is? God, I should have stayed on base. I'm going up to get changed.'

While her husband marched into the house, Jilly dropped to her knees to remove her son's army boots. When they were off, she led him inside, casting a slightly embarrassed smile Midge's way in passing.

EIGHT

She was dreaming of the old cottages, but in the dream the weeds and ivy were gone and they had roofs and doors, and windows with curtains. Every dwelling looked eminently habitable, yet there was no one about, until, in the distance, a figure – a boy – walked round the corner of a house. At sight of her he stopped abruptly; stared back at her. Too far off for her to get a good look at him, she started towards him, but then – *rap-rap-rap* – 'Midge, sorry to wake you, telegram from your mum, thought you'd want to see it right away.'

She sat up fast, the dream behind her.

'Telegram? What's wrong?'

Inger approached, bearing a sheet of paper. 'Don't panic, it's just a communication to keep us up to date. I hate telegrams, though. So terse.'

Midge read the telegram.

DEAR ALL. INANIANS PROVING DIFFICULT, BUT WILL
SPOIL THEIR FUN IF THEY DON'T BLAST US OUT OF WATER
FIRST. HOPE ALL WELL THERE. LOVE MALENA AND DAVE.
KISSES TO MIDGE.

She had barely finished when Inger, returning to the
door, said: 'Oh, do you think you could avoid using
the lav for a while?'

Midge looked up. 'What?'

'It's blocked. Happens sometimes. Victorian
plumbing. Shouldn't be too long. I've called a man to fix
it. Name of Underwood.'

The door closed. Midge read the telegram again, then
a third time before getting out of bed and casting about
for somewhere to lodge it. Her mother sometimes stuck
postcards and other small printed items in the corners of
picture frames. Well, plenty of those here. She folded
the telegram and was slotting it into one of the thin
black frames on the wall when she noticed that the
picture within the frame was of the row of cottages she'd
walked among two days earlier, except that in the
picture they weren't ruined. Her dream came back to

her. She'd dreamt of them as they looked here, with upper floors and roofs, smoke lazing out of chimneys, small gardens that ended at the gated wall. A horse and cart stood outside the wall, and there were women and girls in long skirts, a couple of men in bowler hats, hands in pockets, loitering for the camera. At the bottom of the picture, handwritten in faded brown ink, was a caption: 'Post Office Row'.

She looked at the next picture along: Rouklye church viewed from below the steps where she'd waited for Juby. Unlike the cottages, the church in the photo looked much the same in the present day, but the third picture – of a massive vine-covered house standing four-square in well-tended grounds bound by a high brick wall – was another story entirely. According to the writing underneath, this was the rectory. The rectory Juby had shown her was a grey husk of a building that ended abruptly where the first floor had once begun. The broad doors were gone, the enormous windows reduced to empty rectangles, the walls of the great rooms stripped back to bare stone, while the neat paths and fine gardens had become a featureless tract of open ground without one flower, bush or shrub.

She glided along to the next picture, and the next, the next, all down the line, straightening them as she went without thinking. Some showed bits of countryside she hadn't seen, or the coast she had yet to visit, but most were of houses and cottages that were either ruined now or no longer existed in any form. Every property had a name, or the names of the people who were living there when the picture was taken, written on small rectangles of yellowing card, occasionally with a scrap of information about them. She discovered, for instance, that Stile Cottage had stood above a place called Thorn Hollow, that a family by the name of Warren had lived there for a time, and that Cowleaze, a bungalow, had been built in 1910 by the Mulliner family for use as a summer residence. And there was Brooker's Thatch. No information about this one, but could it be the home of Billy Brooker, whose picture she'd seen above the pegs in the schoolhouse? The Billy Brooker who drowned at the age of seventeen?

The last two photos were of a more imposing property than any but the Rectory. The captions below both of these read 'Rouklye Great House'. In the garden of one, a girl of seven or eight stood in a white pinafore dress holding a tennis racket. Midge wondered who she was and how she'd ended up. Was she still alive, an old biddy in a wheelchair eking out a pension in some anonymous bungalow, constantly comparing life today with how it used to be, at the Great House when she was young? Recalling her previous contempt for these photos, Midge was ashamed. Turning from the last of them, she caught the Midge in the mirror, also turning, and could not meet her eye.

Stepping out of range of the mirror, she bumped into the little table containing the wooden chess set. Several of the pieces toppled over. She knew nothing about chess, but putting the pieces back on the right squares was a simple matter of copying the arrangement of the opposing pieces. Like the photos on the wall and the bits of crude rock dotted about the room, she hadn't given the chess set more than a cursory glance before. But now that she looked at it properly she saw how well-made it was, though it had a hand-carved look about it. It was made from two kinds of wood, half the squares and one set of pieces being fairly light in colour, the rest as black as jet. The whole thing needed dusting. She wiped one of the chessmen with a tissue. It glowed gratefully. She considered polishing the rest, but decided there wasn't much point as it wasn't a complete set. She wondered where the missing piece had got to. It was one of the black corner pieces with battlements on top. Maybe she would ask Inger what had happened to it. Maybe she wouldn't.

She got dressed and opened the door to go down to breakfast just as Edwin came strolling along the landing in blue rubber gloves, a Rupert Bear scarf knotted behind his neck. He carried a large rubber plunger.

'Crapper,' he said as he went by.

'Pardon?' said Midge.

'Tommy Crapper. Bog-maker to Queen Victoria. And us. Haven't you noticed his logo on the pan?' He entered the smallest room at the end of the landing. 'Funny the things people choose to invent, isn't it? I mean Mr C might have pioneered the motor car, the deckchair, anything at all. A range of sweets even. You can see it, can't you? Crapper's Liquorice Allsorts. Crap sweets for short.'

He got down on his knees in front of the large white bowl, tugged the scarf up over his nose, and inserted the plunger.

'But no,' he went on, muffled by the scarf. 'He woke up one morning and said to himself, "I know, I'll go into flush toilets!" Just as well really, or who knows what I'd have been doing to pass the time this fine morning. You know, I sometimes wonder if I took a wrong turn in my youth. Had a fancy to sail the seven seas, be a dashing adventurer, great lover of tall women with no agenda. Instead I became a ledger clerk, hardly looked up from a desk for forty-five years, and here I am today, henpecked, pensioned off, arm down a U-bend. You have to laugh.'

Hoping he wouldn't be in there all day, Midge descended the stairs, into a pall of black smoke.

Inger Bjølstad was happy to admit to anyone who cared that she was no cook. The preparation of meals, she had decided long ago, was what Edwin was for. For the most part, Edwin went along with this assessment, but once or twice in a pale blue moon he rebelled and dialled a pizza or curry. Inger couldn't stand either, which added to his pleasure. His kitchen-manager role had started some twenty-five years ago when he enrolled in a Mediterranean Cookery course. Pleased with his results he had followed this with Italian Regional Cookery, English Home Cooking, and (Inger's idea) Norwegian Cuisine. In spite of all this coaching Edwin wouldn't have got his own TV series, but he was happy enough, generally, to tie a bow in the apron Inger had given him one Christmas, years ago. Just as well, or he wouldn't have eaten. Inger could rustle up a fair breakfast cereal when pressed, but her culinary expertise ended there. Toast was a particular problem for her. The trouble with toast was that it had a way of burning itself to a crisp while she stood gazing out of the window or leaning on the table browsing through *The Times*. Fortunately, she preferred her toast a little on the dark side; fine for her if rather less so for those with more delicate palates and a full set of working nostrils.

Midge's eyes smarted as she spluttered through the swirling smog and reached for the packet of Bran Flakes. Inger drew her attention to the row of charred relics in the toast rack.

'I've scraped a couple specially for you.'

'No thanks.' She opened the fridge door. 'Any milk?'

'Last drop went in my tea, sorry. Not sure if today's has been delivered yet. That milkman, he turns up whenever he pleases.'

'I'll go and look.'

She went out to the step, and gulped gratefully at the clean air. The milk was there, two bottles, the caps already delved into by birds. A printed note was tucked between them, not from the birds.

It is regretted that due to falling demand and increased costs, bottled milk will no longer be delivered from September 13. From that date milk will be delivered in cartons at a slightly revised price, about which customers will be notified shortly.

She folded the note, picked up the bottles.

'Morning, Evy! What's happening over there on the sunny side of the street?'

Juby Bench, leaning out of his window at The Ferryman. She glanced about her. The street was empty but there were houses on both sides, and people in them, with ears. She held the bottles up.

'I'm just fetching the milk.' A shouted whisper. A curtain twitched.

'Had your brekkers?' Juby bawled back.

'Just going to.' She edged towards the door.

'They do a good breakfast here! Keep you going all day, breakfasts at The Ferryman! Why don't you join me?'

She considered pretending that she hadn't heard this and rushing back indoors, but –

'Yeah, good idea! Come over! And bring the old girl! I'll just get into my pants and put a comb through me hair! Fifteen minutes, dining room, see you there!'

He ducked inside and Midge went back into the house wishing she hadn't gone for the milk.

The windows were open in the kitchen, but it was another still day and the air wasn't in a wafting mood. Inger now sat at the epicentre of the fog spreading *Mackay's Dundee Orange Marmalade* on black toast. When Midge dropped the dairy's note on the table, she read it with disdain.

'It had to happen. Pity. I like my bottles, even if the blasted birds do get to them first. And "slightly revised price"! We know what that means, don't we? We'll be paying more for dreadful little cardboard boxes that can't be opened without milk sloshing everywhere.'

She screwed up the note and tossed it over her shoulder.

'I just saw Juby,' Midge said. 'He invited us over for breakfast.'

'I heard. All Steepridge heard. I'm already having mine.' A finger and thumb dropped the corner of toast and she gulped at a mug of tea. 'You go. I'll try and make it another time, tell him.'

'But I can't go on my own!'

Inger looked up. Smiled at her with charcoaled teeth.

'Course you can. Juby's not an ogre. He just looks like one.'

NINE

Inside The Ferryman, behind a high oak counter that gleamed with polished age, a young woman in a neat white blouse looked up from the staff rota she was examining.

'Help you?'

'I'm here to see Mr Bench,' Midge said. When the receptionist's blank expression suggested a need for further information, she added, 'He told me to come over for breakfast.'

'Oh, you're visiting a resident. What name again?'

'Mr Bench. Juby Bench.'

'Bench...' The woman ran a finger down the register. 'My first morning back from holiday, not sure who's... Ah! J.S. Bench.' She looked up. 'You're sure he's expecting you?'

'Yes.'

'I'll ring through to his room, tell him you're here.'

A small panic. 'No, it's all right, I'll wait, he said the dining room, fifteen minutes, it must be about that.'

'He probably meant the Breakfast Room.' The receptionist pointed through a lofty archway, beyond which Midge could see square tables covered in white cloths. 'If you wait there, Mr Rackham will look after you.'

She crossed the floral-carpeted hall, wishing Juby hadn't invited her. The kitchen smog would have been preferable to this place, with its musty smell, its red flock wallpaper, the antlered head staring from the wall. She felt silly here. So absolutely, *unutterably* out of place.

'Evy!'

She jumped; glanced towards the broad staircase to her right: Juby, in his black suit, which looked so rumpled today that he might have slept in it.

'Where's Inger?' he asked as he joined her.

'She was already eating. Said another time.'

'Come on then, let's you and me go and pad ourselves out a bit.'

He strode into the Breakfast Room and she followed. It wasn't a large room. There were only eight tables, two of which were occupied by couples, one quite elderly, reading newspapers while they ate, the other in their early 20s, grinning at one another as Mr Rackham, the proprietor, finished serving them.

'Morning, Reg,' Juby said. 'Table for two today. Have you met my guest? Miss Evy Miller. Inger and Ed's granddaughter.'

'How do you do,' Mr Rackham said with a small bow, and, to Juby: 'Where would you like to sit?'

'The window, as usual.'

They went to the window table, where Midge was about to seat herself when she felt the chair being eased in beneath her from behind, and half rode on it, the thick tablecloth brushing her legs. Juby seated himself across from her, without Mr Rackham's assistance. Then they were each handed a small menu card.

'Leave you for a minute?' he asked.

'A minute should do it,' said Juby.

Midge settled her elbows on the table so that the little menu was on a level with her eyes, and peeped over it at her host. It wasn't only his suit that was rumpled this morning. His face was corrugated with lines, he hadn't shaved, and if he'd combed his hair as he said he was going to it hadn't made much difference. The hair she could sympathise with. The only time hers looked reasonable was when she was climbing out of the chair at the hairdresser's. Almost always, in the street 30 seconds later, it was all over the place again.

'Dunno why I look at this,' Juby said, dropping the menu. 'Always have the Full English at The Ferryman. You don't see many Full Englishes in Germany. The *child's* Full English here is like the adult's in most places. Not that I'm suggesting you have the child's, of course.'

On principle she avoided the Children's Menu in the bottom right hand corner, but a glance at the components of the Full English Breakfast (adult's) brought a gasp.

'I can't eat this much!'

'Sure you can.'

'And I've never had fried bread.'

'Never had fried bread? Everybody's had fried bread.'

'I haven't. And...' – she hesitated, not wanting to sound fussy – 'I don't really like mushrooms.'

'No problem. All the rest though? Leave what you can't manage for Reg's cats.'

He inclined his head and Mr Rackham came over. Juby ordered an extra sausage for Midge in place of the mushrooms, and for himself the standard Full English (adult's).

'Come on,' he said when they were alone, 'let's get our starters.'

'Starters? As well?'

Juby laughed. 'I'm a growing lad, you're a growing gal!'

He shoved his chair back and Midge followed him to a large framed print – blue from years of exposure to direct sunlight – of a three-masted schooner in a storm. On a table below the picture there was an assortment of single-portion cereal packets and two glass jugs, one containing milk, the other orange juice. Juby poured them each a tumbler of orange and broke two boxes of cereal into an inadequate white bowl for himself. Midge also took a bowl, but contented herself with a single portion of *Frosties*. The milk jug was enormous and so full that it required both of her hands to lift it.

She followed Juby back to the table, trying not to spill the contents of her glass and bowl. Once they were seated, Juby plugged his face with a heaped spoonful and began to crunch noisily while Midge set about her cereal with an elegance that would have surprised her parents. Feeling far from right breakfasting with an old man in a hotel, she imagined that all eyes and thoughts must be on her. She glanced around. The young couple were too involved in one another to wonder about her, but the male half of the elderly pair was whispering to his wife, who smiled uncertainly at Midge. She turned to the bay window. There wasn't much of a garden beyond it, just a rectangle of crazy-paving within a sun-beaten border of stunted flowers, and two large black dustbins. The lid of one of the bins had fallen off and lay upside down on the ground. A ginger cat stood on the lid, tugging at a strip of bacon that was stuck to it.

'What you doing today then?' Midge asked when the crunchy silence became too much for her.

Juby shrugged. 'Same as yesterday, same as the day before, same as tomorrow, all being well.'

'Rouklye?'

'Course.'

'You go there every day?'

'It's what I come over for.'

'But there's nothing there.'

'There's enough.' He polished off his cereal in two final mouthfuls. 'Thought I'd head out to Crowbarrow today. Get me some sea air.'

'Sea air?'

At once she was visualising salt water on shingle, gulls wheeling overhead, feeling sand between her toes, unaware that her breakfast companion was watching her with those searching eyes of his.

'You like the sea, Evy?'

'Yes.'

'You can't come with me,' he said.

She look up at him; frowned. 'I didn't ask to.'

He sat back. 'No, no, that'd never do.'

She returned to her cereal. 'Things to do here anyway.'

He ruminated for a few moments, probing the gaps between his teeth with the tip of his tongue.

'Some terrible people about these days,' he said at last.

'Mm,' she agreed.

'I could be one of them. Besides, I go on a bit, I know I do. 'Bout the past and all. And I'm not only going to the sea. Be walking all over, anywhere that's not restricted. I won't be rushing back.'

'Don't worry about it,' she said, chasing the last of the *Frosties* round her bowl.

Juby gazed at her bowed head, her drooping shoulders, and, though she didn't see it, his expression softened.

'You know, you remind me of someone.'

She looked up. 'I do? Who?'

'Not sure. The boy maybe.' Before she could ask what boy, he said: 'You'll have to clear it with your grandparents.'

'Clear what?'

'You coming with me.'

'I thought I couldn't.'

'You want to or don't you?'

'Well,' she said evasively.

'Long as you can put up with being seen with me. And bored rigid.'

'I'll chance it.'

'Better take something to read in case.'

'I haven't got anything to read.'

'I seem to remember there's a bookshop not far from where you're staying.'

'I'm not a great reader.'

'Up to you,' he said. 'But only if you get their say-so.'

'I'll ask Gran.' Mr Rackham arrived with their plates. Midge gaped at the food mountain he set before her. 'Right after breakfast.'

TEN

Juby's car was as worn and scruffy as its owner, but surprisingly comfortable. Midge stretched up in the passenger seat as they drove out of Steepridge to see if she could reach the roof with the top of her head. She couldn't, quite, unlike the driver, who was obliged to sit hunched over the wheel. Whenever they went over a bump there was a dull thud, followed by a small grunt, as his skull introduced itself to the roof. He never remarked on this, or even seemed aware of it. She had to ask.

'This car.'

'What about it?' Juby said.

'It's got a very low roof for a tall person.'

'Oh, I don't know.'

'You don't think you'd be better off with a bigger one?'

'Bigger what?'

'Car. Then you could sit up straight.'

'I am sitting up straight.'

'No you're not.'

He glanced at each of his shoulders in turn, bunched up round his ears. 'You know, you're right. I never noticed.'

'How long have you had it?' Midge said. 'The car.'

'Oh, years. Almost from new.'

'You bought it almost from new and you didn't notice you had to crouch over the wheel to drive?'

'Can't say I did. Funny, that.'

The car park wasn't nearly as crowded this time, it being early in the day for most visitors. They might have arrived sooner still if Inger hadn't insisted on making sandwiches for the pair of them and a flask of tea for Juby. 'I don't know what Edwin will say when he hears,' she said as she arranged the refreshments in a canvas shoulder bag.

'About what?' Midge asked.

'You going there with Juby again – and without me to keep his feet on the ground.'

'Feet on the ground?'

'Oh, it's just one of the many bees in my old man's bonnet.'

When they got out of the car, the sun slapped them hard. Midge scowled at the harsh light. She'd forgotten her sunglasses again. Juby didn't wear sunglasses. He felt the heat, though, and threw his jacket across the back seat. Inger's insistence that her granddaughter coat her exposed parts with a sun block factor 30 had been a wise precaution. Juby obviously didn't bother with sun blocks of any factor. His skin looked as if it were made of the same old brown leather as his car seats – but when he fell against the vehicle on the driver's side he was instantly so ashen that even the leathery tan seemed to have drained away.

'What's up?' she asked, going round the car.

'Nothing. Must have got out of that crouch too quickly.'

He gave it a few moments more before reaching in for the refreshment bag, then slammed the door and strode away without locking it.

This time he headed not down to the village but in the opposite direction entirely, towards the top end of the car park. The faded blue short-sleeved shirt he wore today wasn't much less rumpled than his saggy-bottomed trousers, and he still wore the sandals that had seen better days. Comparing their attire, Midge felt far too smart in her crisp white top and cerise shorts.

'You know what?' Juby said, to himself apparently, for she was walking some way behind him. She sped up to catch the rest. 'They have a Conservation Officer who travels the country giving slide shows and lectures about the wonderful work the Ministry of Destruction does on the land it's stolen. They even have their own magazine, praising their efforts in protecting wildlife, nature and all. And what do you think they call it? "Sanctuary". Sanctuary! If you ever want to know the meaning of the word hypocrisy, look no further.'

Looking neither to right nor left as he walked, he did not see a white Toyota sweep in from the road. Midge grabbed his arm and pulled him to a halt.

'Watch out!'

He stared at her hand, then her face. 'What?'

'That.'

She released him and indicated the car, which had stopped inches from him. Juby glanced blankly at the Toyota and the scowling driver behind the windscreen, and walked on. Again Midge hurried after him. He continued speaking as though there'd been no interruption.

'This valley was a wildlife preserve for centuries before the uniforms moved in with their tanks and explosives, their barbed-wire and all. Wasn't called that, of course; it was just the way of things. Protecting nature? They wouldn't know nature if it flapped in their face and beaked their eyes out. Nature means natural. Tell me what's natural about fencing species off from one another, human or animal.'

'But you keep coming back,' Midge said.

'Yes, I do, don't I? Well, never again. Last time, this.'

'Today, you mean?'

'Last trip. Ever. Look at that.'

His 'Look at that' was for the list of dos, don'ts and requests printed on the large noticeboard they'd come to at the edge of the car park.

YOU ARE NOT ALLOWED TO
TRADE, LIGHT FIRES, STAY OVERNIGHT
OR CYCLE ON THE WALKS.
PLEASE TAKE YOUR LITTER HOME
AND KEEP DOGS UNDER CONTROL.
DO NOT USE METAL DETECTORS.
ENJOY THE WONDERFUL VIEWS.

'Or else,' Juby said, walking on.

Beyond the car park, woods contained by barbed-wire and slat-fencing stretched away far to the right and a little to the left, the two bulging parts separated by a track just wide enough for a single vehicle, though another notice, much smaller than the first, stated that no civilian transport was allowed here. Some way into the twin shadows of the divided wood the track became a bridge over a shallow brook. Here Juby paused, and, naturally, Midge paused with him.

'Listen,' he said.

She did so. 'All I can hear is the water.'

'That's right.'

'So…?'

'Used to be a lot more than the sound of water. Thick with birds, these woods were. All the Rouklye woods, all sorts of birds. Hear 'em all day long, from before dawn to past dark. And the rooks. I loved those birds. Their croaky old voices. Antisocial creatures, they say, but they like to be near farms, villages, people. That doesn't strike me as so antisocial, does it you?'

His gaze drifted among the upper branches of the silent trees.

'After we were given the push I snuck back a few times and they were gone, every last one of them. Rooks here for centuries – that's where the place got its name, they say – but I never saw nor heard a one from the day they kicked us out. Y'know, I always had this idea that if the rooks came back, if just one returned…'

She waited, but there was nothing more except a sharp sniff – the kind that puts a categorical end to sentimental notions – after which he withdrew his gaze from the birdless trees and continued across the bridge. As ever, she followed, like some incidental accessory.

At the end of the track a vertical slab that greatly resembled a tombstone gave visitors a choice of direction: to the right Crowbarrow Bay, while ahead, over a cattle grid, a footpath through an overgrown meadow rose to meet the sky and a range of cliffs. At the head of this path a further notice instructed visitors to keep within the yellow markers that bordered it.

'Four hundred feet above sea level at their peak, those cliffs,' Juby said. 'When I was a lad I walked along them all the time, along 'em and down to the cove. Good weather, I'd strip off and have me a nice dip down there.'

'You won't be doing that today, will you?' she said.

He snorted. 'If I did they'd probably stand me against a rock and shoot me. This way.'

He started along the track to Crowbarrow. Again, she had to get a move on to catch and keep up with him. She asked how far it was.

'Two thirds of a mile. No distance.'

The fenced-off woods ran along the right-hand side of the track, while the rising meadow to their left became a long hill on which three armoured tanks sat. The tanks weren't moving and Midge assumed that they were unoccupied. Hoped they were. Those great barrels looked as if they might swivel at a moment's notice and blast her into the woods. Also on the hill stood a series of enormous black boards, each bearing a single red numeral:

4   5   6   7

'What are they for?' she asked.

'You've heard of painting-by-numbers?' Juby said. 'Well, round here they have blowing-up-hills-by-numbers.'

The sun beat down mercilessly from an opaque blue sky, uncluttered but for a handful of fluffy white strands feathering across it. After some fifty yards, they heard a motor behind them and moved out of the way. A khaki-coloured Land Rover with crimson stripes bumped by, kicking up dust and small stones.

'Range warden,' Juby hissed, in a way that said 'Watch yourself: Authority'. When he then cupped his hands and shouted 'Making sure we behave ourselves!' Midge nervously eyed the tanks on the hill. When the Land Rover skidded to an immediate halt, her legs nearly gave way.

But the warden hadn't stopped to respond to Juby's taunt. Jumping out of the vehicle, he knelt to inspect a stretch of fencing that had come away. "Nother fine day,' he said cheerily as they drew level.

Juby grunted and stopped to watch him twist the wire with a pair of pliers. Midge lurked anxiously in the background. 'My young friend here,' Juby said to the man's back, 'was wondering why the woods are out-of-bounds.'

'I wasn't,' she protested, but quietly.

The warden looked round. 'Several reasons,' he said to her. 'Some rare flowers in there for one.'

'And for another?' Juby pursued with exaggerated innocence.

The man stood up, gave him an I-know-what-you're-after look, and rattled about among his tools in the Land Rover. Then, hammer in hand, he again addressed Midge.

'Thousands of tank shells are fired on the range every year and there's always a few that don't go off. Some land in the sea, some on the hills, some in the woods. With the best will in the world we can't keep track of them all. The fences are a safety precaution.'

She glanced apprehensively at the way ahead.

'Don't worry,' the warden said. 'All access points are swept for unexploded devices before the public's let in.

94

You'll be all right as long as you don't go where you're not supposed to.'

He gave the fence post a couple of thumps with the hammer, tugged it this way and that to make sure it wouldn't move, and climbed back into his vehicle. Then, waving an arm out the door, he sped off along the track.

Midge soon discovered that two thirds of a mile is a long way for near strangers of very different generations to walk together. When the last of the chit-chat had dried up, they trudged in silence. Glad of any distraction, she was relieved when she heard a brisk footfall close behind. She looked round, ready to step aside if need be to let whoever it was go by.

There was no one there.

Yet the footsteps continued, passed by, went on ahead of them. She tried to speak, but could only gulp, repeatedly. Juby, a few paces ahead, glanced back.

'Whassup?'

'Did you hear that?' she managed in a tight little voice.

'Hear what?'

'F – footsteps.'

For a second she thought he was about to smile, but he didn't, quite, or even pass comment, merely continued walking. Not wanting to be alone, and determined to forget what she'd heard, she rushed after him.

In a minute, Juby said: 'Tell me about Miss Miller.'

'Miss Miller?'

'That is you, isn't it?'

'There's nothing to tell.'

'There's always something to tell. You've got a home, haven't you? You have friends, interests, likes and dislikes.'

She ransacked her brain for something to say about herself that wasn't too personal and blurted a smattering of self-conscious scraps that gave little away and sounded so dull that even she was bored.

'Your turn,' she said when she was done.

'My turn?'

'To tell me about you.'

'I wouldn't know where to start,' he said gruffly.

Keener to reverse their roles than learn more about him, she said: 'It doesn't matter where.'

He reflected for a few paces, before: 'Polynesian nose-flutes.'

'What?'

'I used to play them. For the rent, food, ciggies and so on. I smoked then. Rolled me own. I'm talking about the nineteen-fifties. That's how I met Inger. Busking in Amsterdam.'

She gaped. 'You met my gran in Amsterdam? Busking?'

'There I was, playing my nose off on this street corner,'

Juby said, 'and along comes this dark-haired beauty in shorts up to here, drops a few coppers in me cap, and we get to talking, she buys me a meal, and...' He smiled, and left it at that.

'And that was her?'

'That was her. She'd not long graduated from university in Oslo. On a solo walking tour to get all the work out of her system, in no hurry, so she stuck around and I showed her how to play the nose-flutes.'

'Nose-flutes! You're making it up.'

'Making it up?' he said. 'I'll have you know I did very well with the flutes on the streets of Europe. Amsterdam, Brussels, Paris, Berlin, I did 'em all. Inger, though, she didn't really have the nose. Couldn't get the hang of breathing out with a pipe up each nostril. It's an art.'

'It'd have to be. What happened after you met?'

'Well, I'd been out of England for the best part of a decade, and it'd been on my mind to pop back and see how the old place was getting on without me, and as she wasn't working to a strict route or schedule she said she'd tag along. We hiked down through Holland, across Belgium, top end of France, and from there to Dover. A ferry helped with that bit.'

'A fairy?'

'A boat. For the water. Made a good team, Inger and

me. We could keep pace with one another, had plenty to talk about, never fell out...'

He trailed off, back in the old days with lithe young Inger Bjølstad.

'Just good friends, I suppose,' Midge said.

He chuckled. 'It was a long walk.'

Thanks to the irregular lie of the land, no matter how far they went the sea never quite revealed itself, but when they had walked about three quarters of the way Juby began pointing out where this or that dwelling once stood: beside the track, amid the trees, in that dip, up there in a fold of the hillside. Of most there remained nothing more than a ragged line of stones, or a door-frame supported by a bit of crumbling wall, while others had vanished entirely. He had a name for almost every building, whether there was anything left of it or not, a few of which she recalled from the captions on the photos in her room: Stile Cottage, Cutting Cottage, Chine House. Juby waved an arm in the direction of a line of tumbled stones.

'Brooker's Thatch,' he said. 'The "thatch" was because of the roof. Risky thing out here, thatch, the gales on this part of the coast.'

'Brooker's Thatch?' Midge said. 'Would that be where Billy Brooker lived?'

He glanced at her. 'Where did you hear of Billy Brooker?'

'He was in a photo in the school room.'

'Billy was way before my time, but I remember his folks, and his sisters. The Brookers kept a few cows out here, a few more down in the village, near the Rectory. Had a man take the milk round in pails, door to door, ladling it out by the pint. No milk bottles then.'

'None now either, soon,' she muttered.

'Now there's a sight on a day like this!' Juby said suddenly.

She'd been walking the final stretch sideways, picking out the remnants of Brooker's Thatch, gazed at mere hours ago as a complete building in a thin black frame. Turning to see what Juby had referred to, she saw that the hill to their left had declined sharply into a dazzling blue expanse contained within the horseshoe of Crowbarrow Bay. Her eyes lit up. At last!

But then...

A feeling to one side of her, a very powerful feeling, of having been joined by another. She turned. A ragged-haired youth stood a couple of yards away, gazing at the sea in a rapture that reflected her own of a moment before. Where had he sprung from? She looked harder. She'd seen him before, quite recently.

A momentary turmoil while she tried to remember. Then she had it. The schoolroom, that first visit. The second silhouette, sitting across from Juby at the end window. It had to be him, with that profile. But now that he stood before her in the full light of day she saw how like the old man he was. Dead-ringer, in fact – as Juby might have looked in his teens. He even had his nose, in embryo.

'Er...'

It was meant as a tug to Juby, who'd continued walking a little way and now stood, like the boy, gazing out to sea. He didn't hear, but the boy must have, for he looked at her in surprise, as though only now aware of her. He opened his mouth to speak.

And faded out of existence.

ELEVEN

It wasn't until the boy vanished that Midge realised that he'd not appeared to be wholly there anyway. She hadn't been able to see through him exactly, but there'd certainly been something rather less than substantial about him. A ghost? In broad daylight? Shocked rather than frightened by the apparition, she advanced on Juby, intending to tell him what she'd seen; but he began to speak at the sound of her approach.

'Good few ships have gone down around this bay over the years,' he said. 'There was a coastguard station and a signal canon on the Tout till 1910 or thereabouts, but there were still wrecks.'

The moment was past. She shook the almost-there boy away in favour of the immediate, ever-visible world.

'What's the Tout?' she asked, drawing level with her guide.

He gestured to the far left of the bay, a steep promontory. 'Old name for those rocks. Means lookout point. Stand there and look east on a day like today and you can see all the way to St Aldhelm's Head. Look the other way and you'll see Arish Mell, Mupe Bay, and more. Up there's where Davy Miller's house stood,' he added, changing the subject so swiftly that it took a second for her to become aware of it.

'Davy Miller?' she said then.

He looked at her. 'Yes, why? Name mean something?'

'It's my dad's name. Only he's usually called Dave.'

'Oh yes, I was forgetting. You're a Miller. Know much about the Millers of Crowbarrow, do you?'

'I've never heard of them.'

'Really? I'd have thought someone would have mentioned them, your dad being of their stock and all.'

'Dad's not big on family history. Believes in the future, not what's gone, he's always saying that.'

'And you?'

'Me?'

'All future, no past?'

She had no answer to this. 'These Millers of Crowbarrow...'

An invitation to speak of them. Juby obliged.

'The Crowbarrow Millers were a fishing family. Sort of a clan really. As much a part of this stretch as the fossils you can turn up with a spade a little way along. Don't suppose it ever crossed their minds that they'd be forced out of here, but then in a matter of weeks they weren't even neighbours any more, and the coast they'd lived by for generations was barred to them.'

'And they were definitely relatives of my dad's?'

'And yours,' Juby said.

'Mine?'

'Well, if you're his daughter...'

She shook her head in disbelief. How could she know nothing of these people if she was related to them?

'Can you tell me anything else about them?'

'Like what?'

'I don't know, what is there?'

'Well, there's Davy, like I said. His house, being tucked away in that nook there, was sheltered from the worst of the gales, and had the best views around. Caught every sunrise and sunset, his place.'

'Any others?'

'Millers, you mean?'

'Yes.'

'Stacks,' Juby said. 'The ones that stood out for me

were the brothers, Ethan, Seth and Enoch. Enoch was famous for his fingers. Had five on each hand.'

'Doesn't everyone?'

'Everyone else has four fingers and a thumb. Enoch had a thumb plus five fingers. The fifth was a little one tagged on the end, beside the next smallest, which earned him the nickname Sixer. He didn't seem to mind. Hell of a fisherman, old Enoch. Then there was Granny Fleur, Londoner originally, mother of Iris and Lily. Iris was married to Ethan...no, I tell a lie, Ethan never married. Iris was Seth's missus. Enoch didn't marry either, but he lived with a woman called Joan, who made fancy hats that she sold at Wareham market. Another branch of the Millers lived up there, on the—'

He continued in this vein, cataloguing Miller after Miller, where their homes had stood, the names of their partners and children, and soon Midge was barely listening as she imagined all those hitherto unknown relatives going about their lives here, taking the boats out, hauling the fish in, their kids running along the shore where only day-visitors and Army personnel came today. It was so still here now. So lifeless. Bleak almost. There weren't even any gulls. Scared off decades ago maybe, by the guns and shellfire that must be deafening when the range was closed to the public.

'Here's something,' Juby said. She made herself pay attention. 'When the War Office decided they needed the valley, they sent a letter to all the householders giving them a month's notice. Had to be gone by the week before Christmas, it said, and no buts. Signed by a Major-General Miller of Southern Command.'

'One of these Millers?'

'If he was, no one claimed him. Coincidence, I expect, but an extra twist of the knife for the Crowbarrow branch. Most of them, like the Rouklye villagers, felt it their patriotic duty to quit without fuss because they'd been told it was in the nation's interests, but it was too much for some. Old Davy now. They loaded him and Mrs Davy on a lorry with all their gear and dropped them off at some dump that had been found for them out Stoborough way. Davy breathed his last a week after the move, begging to be brought back. Mind you, he did have the flu, and he was in his ninetie—'

He broke off abruptly, an odd dry sound rattling in his throat. He sagged, staggered backwards groping for something to lean on.

'What is it?' Midge said. 'What's wrong?'

Juby found a fence post and jammed his lower back against it, eyes screwed up tight. The colour had once again drained from his face. Midge cast about for help – a summer visitor who just happened to be a doctor or nurse, someone, anyone, who could take charge – but there was only her, and the best she could do was fret and dither helplessly for the two or three minutes it took Juby to open his eyes again. Red-rimmed, watery eyes.

'All right now?' she asked.

He cleared his throat. 'Touch of the heat, is all.'

His voice was taut, strained, gravely. Tugging his tea-towel of a hanky from his pocket to mop his neck and brow, he failed to notice the small object that flew out with it. Midge stooped, picked it up, turned it over in her hand. It was a carved wooden chess piece, as smooth and shiny as a new conker, jet black, with battlements on top. The missing corner piece from the set in her room – had to be!

'What's that you've got there?' Juby asked.

She held the chessman out to him. 'You dropped it.'

He took it from her. 'My talisman. Wouldn't do to lose this, even at this late stage.'

'Talisman?'

'My lucky piece. Always knew I'd come back as long as I had this.' He buffed it up on his sleeve. 'It was Mum's, part of a set she...'

He stopped, and for a moment Midge thought he

was going to have another turn. But he'd paused merely to correct himself.

'I mean Aunty Liss. Edwin's mother. I called her Mum too sometimes.' The admission seemed to embarrass him. 'She taught me to play.'

'Play?'

'Chess.'

'Are you any good?'

'Not really. And out of practice. No one plays back home.'

He shoved his small piece of the past back in his pocket and broached the tricky little path down to the beach. Midge followed, and was soon crunching over pebbles and coarse sand in his heavy-footed wake.

It wasn't much of a beach, and there weren't many people on it: a few strollers, three or four families some way along, and in the water just two, a young woman with her small naked child, a pretty little thing with bright blonde curls, lifting her legs high and squealing as the surf hissed about her. The water looked so inviting that Midge slipped her sandals off and ran straight in – and straight out again, screaming silently.

'You get used to it!' the woman with the toddler shouted.

The second time she was more prepared, and was

soon up to her knees and splashing water on goosefleshed arms, dabbing her face with her fingertips, shivering exquisitely as icy droplets trickled down her neck.

Juby, too, had entered the water, but no further than the lapping shallows, where the foam fizzed between his bare toes. His sandals lay on the shingle behind him, entwined like exhausted wrestlers. Suddenly he bent double and plunged a hand into the water. Straightening up, he held out his open palm. 'Crowbarrow shells.'

She waded back to look at a small pink and white conch and two brass ammunition cartridges.

'Want them?' he asked.

She would have liked to examine the cartridges at her leisure, maybe take them home as souvenirs, but something made her decline. A look in his eye told her that her refusal pleased him. He closed his hand, drew it back, and lobbed the three shells as far out to sea as they were willing to go.

It was Juby who decided that they should have an early lunch. Settling themselves on a broad flat rock towards the back of the beach, they opened the canvas bag Inger had provided and took out the sandwiches, the flask of tea, Midge's preferred bottle of water, and began to eat and sip. With the salt on her lips and binding the ends of her hair, the sun a golden cloth on her skin, all that stopped it being a perfect moment was the absence of gulls and the overabundance of sand flies that had to be constantly batted away. Like her, Juby said little while he ate, but every so often his eyes would cloud over for reasons she could only guess at.

'If you lived round here,' she said, 'in Steepridge or one of the other villages, you could come here more often. Gran says that apart from August they let people in all through the year, on certain weekends.'

A brusque shake of the head. 'Wouldn't work. Wouldn't ever've worked. Couldn't come and go as I please. No, better to visit once a year like I've been doing. My own terms that way.'

'All right, but why live so far away? Why Germany?'

'It's where my family is.'

'You have a family?'

'Oh yes. Married daughter, three grandkids.'

'Grandchildren?' Hard to imagine him a grandfather.

'Indeed,' he said. 'Two girls, one of ten, one of seven, and the boy, Juby, just turned sixteen. The very age I was when I left here.'

'Juby? Your grandson has the same name as you?'

A dry chuckle. 'I know. German boy with an old West Country name. My daughter's idea. Johanna's a very generous person. I've known many generous women in my life, and I'm glad to say my girl's one of them.'

'Have you ever brought your family here? To Rouklye, Crowbarrow?'

'No. No one's ever expressed much interest. Except the boy. I talk to him about it. He can't get enough of it.' He looked at his large brown hands, a half-eaten sandwich dangling from one of them. 'Good lad, young Jube. Got a letter from him this morning, matter of fact. Must have written it the day I set out, or the day after. He writes well. In English too. Says he's thinking about me here. Isn't that nice?'

'Yes. It is.'

She wondered what might have become of this strange man if he hadn't been forced out of his home all those years ago. With his great beak of a nose, his so-pale blue eyes, the hair just made to be flung around in a gale, he might have forged links with the fishermen of Crowbarrow, joined their ranks even. If the Army hadn't seized the valley and kept it, the cottages around the bay would still be standing, some of them occupied by today's generation of Millers: relatives she might have known and come to visit from time to time. If things had been otherwise she could be sitting here right now watching young cousins running in and out of the water while she listened to the life story of an old Crowbarrow fisherman called Juby Bench.

'What was it like at the end?' she asked.

'The end?'

'Out here, when everyone was leaving.'

'It was cold,' he said, and seemed content to leave it at that.

She offered a prompt: 'Very cold?'

'Bitter. Coldest December in living memory.'

She waited. Another extended pause. 'Go on.'

He did so. 'The sea was icy. Great sheets of spray striking the cliffs. I came here a lot in the last days, saying my goodbyes to the land, the beach. There was a bad storm one night. I stood up there on the cliff through much of it. The valley was mostly clear by the deadline, just a handful still waiting for transport. Then the lorries took the last of us, and that was it. Should have known we wouldn't be coming back. Nothing could have felt more like the end.'

As he finished, Midge's gaze drifted up to the cliffs, and she saw, right on the edge, a tall young figure with a wild mop of hair, staring out to sea.

TWELVE

They returned to the village by an alternative route, on a footpath along the top of the numbered hill they'd paralleled on the trek to Crowbarrow. This was the clifftop hike Juby had mentioned enjoying as a lad. Even for the lad he once was it must have been a bit of a slog, and it was soon obvious that in his early seventies he was far from fit enough to undertake the walk with ease. On the way up the first of what turned out to be just one of many precipitous stretches, Midge asked him what he did in Germany.

'Do?' he said, already breathing hard.

'For a living.'

'Oh, well, these days I live off my pension and the few pennies I've saved.'

'But before?'

'I've been a factory hand, a window-cleaner, road sweeper, painter and decorator, I worked on the odd building site, a few other things. Nothing very impressive.'

'Always in Germany?'

'No, no, all over. Various countries. In Belgium one time I was a clown.'

'A clown?'

'In a circus.'

She laughed. 'You were a circus clown?' It was even more absurd than Edwin being a film extra.

'Only for a month. They sacked me. Said I scared the kids. I used to run up to them and scream in their faces.'

'What did you do that for?'

'Thought it was funny. But there were complaints. The last job I had was as a waiter in a restaurant in Frankfurt. English restaurant. Made out I was German for the tourists. Had great fun with the accent and I had a real gift for looking down my nose at the customers from a great height.'

After this he lapsed into a rasping silence, needing what breath he could grab for the ever-upward trudge. To their right as they climbed, in the grass between the path and the ocean, they passed notice after notice warning them that the cliff was 'unstable'. To their left, set in the ground behind strings of barbed-wire, a series of metal signs bore the words:

**DANGER
UNEXPLODED
SHELLS
KEEP OUT**

'Are you sure we're allowed up here?' Midge asked.

'Course. If we weren't, what'd be the point of the signs?'

'And this is definitely the way back?'

'The path should swing down towards the car park some way along. Always used to anyway. But if they've stuck a barrier somewhere ahead we can always jog down the hill and across the fields.'

'Oh, great. Through the unexploded shells.'

'You worry too much,' Juby said, and puffed on.

After half an hour Midge's clothes were sticking to her and Juby's shirt was wet through. He was very red in the face now, and each breath was drawn as a wheeze, expelled as a gasp. But when she asked him if he wanted to stop for a rest he waved an impatient hand and toiled on, mopping his brow with his enormous hanky. Next time, she made out that it was she who needed the break.

'It's so hot! Can't we sit down for a minute?'

This he could accept – 'Sure, no rush' – it being for her benefit rather than his.

Arduous as the climb was under the relentless sun, the views were an unexpected compensation for Midge, who as a rule had little time for scenery. To one side, beyond the cliff edge, the many luminous blues of the ocean formed an eventual horizon that stretched for miles; on the other, below the hill, beyond the fenced-off woods and scattered remnants of Rouklye village, green and russet hills hemmed the valley. These visual delights aside, she was thankful when Juby's downward route eventually materialised. The path, bordered by yellow markers and notices reminding walkers that it was dangerous to leave it, wended through frayed meadows accessed by weathered stiles and squealing iron gates. For her it was a pleasure to descend, but Juby's breath rasped just as much as before and by the time they reached the cattle grid they'd gazed over before taking the track to Crowbarrow, he looked as if another yard would kill him.

Once within the blessed shade of the bridge through the silent woods, Juby's breathing improved, yet here he became more subdued. After depositing the depleted refreshment bag in the overheated car but showing no inclination to head back to Steepridge, Midge decided to leave him to himself for a bit. While he wandered off on his own, she settled herself on a curved stone seat set into the wall at the church end of Post Office Row. There were trees here, and the shade was again welcome, and as she lolled, eyes closed, bare legs stretched out before her, she felt more content than she had for some time. Every now and then footsteps and voices came and went. She paid no attention to what was said, but, peeking occasionally through her lashes, glimpsed elderly couples or parents with children, and once or twice no one at all. The absence of physical forms to accompany some of the voices did not disturb her unduly. She was getting used to such things here. Besides, she didn't feel threatened by them, any more than she'd felt threatened by the disappearing boy earlier. They were part of the place, along with the ruins, nothing more.

'Popping down to the house, want to come?'

She squinted up at the long streak of darkness with its unruly head in the sun. She would rather have stayed where she was, but he'd invited her to accompany him, which must mean that he wasn't yet sick of her company, so...

'All right.'

She got up and trailed after him, past the schoolhouse

and down the narrow sloping path to his childhood home within its shroud of wire and weeds and warnings.

'See that window?' he said as she joined him, as unaware as last time that while he could see a fair portion of the house she had to stand on tiptoe just to glimpse the top third. 'The upstairs window in the middle.'

'Bit of it,' she said, truthfully enough.

'Some mornings back home, I wake up very early, and I'm in that room, eleven, twelve, thirteen years old. My eyes are still shut, but I know it's just getting light, and I lie there waiting for the first bird to start up. Then it comes, this single sound, and then there's a warble from another quarter, and a whistle, a shriek, a flap of feathers, till there's a hundred of 'em, might be a thousand, and the woods are bursting with their unholy racket, and it's like...it's as though...'

She waited, but for Juby words had ceased to be necessary. He was back in his childhood, head tilted, listening to his long dead birds.

Midge listened too. Heard nothing.

THIRTEEN

In theory, meals at her grandparents' were never at a set time. This, according to Inger, was because their lives weren't sliced up into bite-sized portions to fit round television schedules. Edwin had a different view on the timing of meals but kept it to himself, aiming, during weekdays at least, to put food on the table for six-thirty in order to be down the garden in his Pottering Shed for seven. Six-thirty was long gone this evening, however, and as yet there'd been no call to go and eat; but this was fine by Midge, writing to Nessa in her room. She sat at a small table by the window, pausing pen to mouth every now and then, thinking how best to express this or that sensation, describe that or this observation or scene. She wrote about breakfast at The

Ferryman, the walk to the coast, the sweaty hike back along the high cliff. There was quite a lot about Juby, of course: Juby as entertainment for a friend. She also described the derelict bay overlooked by the wretched remains of cottages that might once have housed relatives of hers – and she mentioned the almost-there boy on the track to Crowbarrow. When talking about the boy, she adopted a mildly self-mocking tone so that her friend, if she didn't believe her, wouldn't think she'd lost it. It was the longest letter she'd ever written to anyone, but as she wrote she realised that although she missed Nessa and the company of others her own age it was starting to get a bit more interesting here. 'Anyway,' she said to the chevalier mirror, 'there's always you.' The real Midge Miller smiled smugly back at her, as if to say: 'But of course!'

When she'd filed the finished letter with the one she'd written a few days ago, to post a day or two before Ness got back from holiday, she once again inspected her private picture gallery. Even more of the old photos meant something now. She couldn't place every building, but some of the ones that Juby had pointed out were there, and where the names underneath still meant nothing she thought she recognised that hill, that path, that bit of wall, and this pleased her.

When she was eventually called down for tea at last, by Inger, she found just two places at the table, each containing a portion of Mediterranean Fish Pasta, crisper at the edges than it should have been, each one accompanied by half a tin of warmed-up broad beans, the most tasteless vegetable she could think of.

'Where's Grandpa?'

'Search me,' Inger said. 'He's not talking to me.'

'Why, what have you done?'

'I allowed you to go to Rouklye with Juby again.'

Midge sat down and stared bleakly at her plate. If Edwin had prepared the meal it would probably have been something quite good, and he'd try to make her smile while they were eating, but instead there was this, and he'd gone off in a temper and left an unhappy atmosphere behind him. She tendered a sample of Mediterranean Fish Pasta to her mouth, waited a second or two for her taste buds to leap into action, and decided that it could be worse.

'Gran...'

'Midge, darling, you don't think, do you, that you could experiment with calling me something else? "Gran" has never seemed quite *me* somehow.'

'I wouldn't know what else *to* call you.'

'Try Inger.'

'Oh, I couldn't.' (Not to your face anyway, she thought.)

'Ah well. What was it you wanted to say?'

'You know that chess set in my room?'

'Chess set, chess set,' Inger said, raking her memory. 'Oh, that old thing. Belonged to Larissa. One of the few things she ever gave him.'

'Larissa?'

'Edwin's mother.'

'I never knew her,' Midge said.

'No, she died six or seven years before you were born. I only met her twice myself. Sparky old dame. The chess set was her brother's originally. You don't play, do you? It's years since I played, and Edwin doesn't.'

She shook her head. 'There's a piece missing anyway. That's what I wanted to ask you about.'

'Oh yes, I'd forgotten that. One of the rooks. Even Edwin doesn't know what happened to it.'

'The missing piece isn't a bird,' Midge said. 'It's a castle.'

'The pieces with battlements are usually called rooks,' said Inger.

'Rooks? Are you sure?'

'Of course, why wouldn't I be?'

Midge popped a distracted forkful of fish pasta into her mouth and recalled what Juby had told her on the bridge over the stream as they were setting off for Crowbarrow; how he used to love the sound of the rooks, and that there hadn't been any in the valley since the people were evicted. *I always had this idea that if the rooks came back, if just one returned...* Even at the time she'd been fairly sure what was in his mind: *...if just one returned everything would be all right again.* Was that what he was doing when he came back every year with the chess piece in his pocket, bringing a 'rook' back, as if such a gesture would restore everything? It was on the tip of her tongue to say where the missing piece was, but she bit it back on the grounds that it wasn't her place to do so. Instead she said:

'Juby looks a bit like a rook, don't you think?'

'Juby looks like a chessman?'

'No, the bird. That suit of his, the way he stalks about, even his nose – sort of beak-like.'

Inger laughed. 'Now that you mention it, I think I thought something of the sort myself when I first saw him.'

'In Amsterdam,' Midge said.

'He told you about Amsterdam?'

'Mentioned it.'

'Yes, well there he was with those flute things up his hooter, making a dreadful racket: he was no musician, that young man. But the look of him! Quite the tallest fellow I'd ever seen, and with so much hair – very dark in those days. He wore this long black cape, fastened at the neck with a silver chain – said he'd "borrowed" it from a copper – and he stood on one leg while he played, the other folded up under him somehow. I don't know if rooks stand on one leg, but yes, all in all, very rook-like.'

'He told me he'd been out of England for years, but didn't say why,' Midge said.

Inger traced patterns in her fish pasta with her fork. She seemed to have lost interest in it as food.

'He fled. To avoid conscription.'

'Conscription?'

'In this country, for quite a long time after the war, every able-bodied young man was obliged to spend a couple of years in the armed forces. Juby's call-up papers must have come a year or two after the military took over his precious valley, and nothing would have induced him to join the ranks of the people who'd kicked him out – so he skedaddled to the Continent and didn't come back till the mid-fifties.'

'When you came with him?'

Inger dropped her fork and pushed her plate away. 'For the walk and for my sins, having no idea I would grow senile here. Who knows where I'd be today, what I'd be doing, if he hadn't abandoned me during our day-trip to Rouklye?'

'Day-trip? Abandoned you?'

'Skipped that bit, did he?' Inger said with a half-smile. 'The first thing he wanted to do when we got to Dorset was check out his old stamping ground. He hooked up with Edwin for the first time in years and we both accompanied him. The valley wasn't open to the public then, so we had to go in by a way they used as boys. Edwin hadn't been back since the evacuation, but living locally he had some notion of what to expect. Poor Juby, though, he wasn't prepared at all.'

'For the ruins?'

'They weren't quite ruins then, though from the look of things the buildings had been used for heavy target practice. The US Army had had control of the village in the early days, and by all accounts they treated it with respect, but then the British paras took over...'

'Yes?'

'Well, it was in an unbelievable state. Chimneys toppled; roofs caved in; rusting Army vehicles rammed into walls; litter everywhere; oil drums; bottles; graffiti; excrement and used condoms in former living rooms. Juby was appalled. All those years he'd been imagining

Rouklye as he'd last seen it, and there it was, so bleak, filthy, abused. He turned on his heel and left without a word, to me or anyone else.'

'But you stayed,' Midge said.

'Mm.'

'Why?'

'Because…' Inger sought reasons, clutched straws. 'Because it suited me, because I didn't fancy going all the way back to Norway by myself, because Edwin was rather taken with me…' She crinkled her eyes. 'He made me laugh. I always had a soft spot for men who make me laugh.'

Midge almost remarked that he didn't seem to make her laugh much these days, but resisted. She said: 'When did you see Juby next?'

Instead of answering, Inger sat back in her chair and gazed at her across the table. 'You're very curious all of a sudden. A day or two ago, you didn't seem bothered about anything much, and now you're into life histories. What brings this on?'

Managing, with some effort, not to wilt before her grandmother's bland scrutiny, Midge said: 'Do I have to have a reason?'

Inger gave a half shrug. 'I suppose not.' She took a breath. 'The next time we heard from Juby was the early nineteen-sixties, in a letter from Germany in which he said his wife had passed away. We had no idea he was married till then. He sent a photo. Nice-looking girl. Very lively face. Gabriele, a Swiss, working in Germany when they met, died from a brain haemorrhage. Quite unexpected, apparently, no warning. Simply collapsed one afternoon in the garden. Juby called an ambulance, but it was too late. She was dead on arrival at the hospital.'

'But he stayed in Germany?'

'He had a young daughter at school there. But he started to come over occasionally after Gabriele's death. He would always go to Rouklye, sneak in past the guards. It wasn't until the seventies, when pressure groups finally persuaded the MoD to let the public in every so often, that they began tidying the village up, removing dilapidated roofs, unsafe ceilings, stairs, all the mess they'd made. Since then Juby's visited every August bar four, when he was unwell or needed at home.'

'Have you met his daughter? His grandchildren?'

'No. As far as I know the Müellers have never set foot in England, and Edwin's not a great traveller, so...'

Midge's eyes popped. 'Did you say *Müeller?*'

'His daughter's husband's name and therefore their

children's. It's a fairly common name over there, as Miller is here.'

'Maybe it is,' said Midge. 'But still…'

That night, she dreamed of Rouklye again. Rouklye with all the roofs, windows and doors in place, though again without people. But then, in the dream, the almost-there boy emerged from the post office, looked first one way, then the other, and finally became aware of her. He smiled when he saw her; started towards her, and was almost within reach when she woke with a start, and the boy, and habitable Rouklye, tumbled back into the night.

FOURTEEN

Many of the people who came into the shop were browsers who bought nothing, but most were holidaymakers looking for an undemanding read or something to keep the kids quiet. From the start Inger had encouraged Midge to serve customers, a responsibility she hadn't relished at first but was getting used to and even enjoyed some of the time. Inger was in her office, feet on desk, indulging in one of the four Balkan Sobranie cigarettes she allowed herself each day, when Jilly Barstow entered the shop.

'Hi, Midge. Busy helping Granny?'

'*Granny?*' Inger bellowed. Her head jumped up in the hatch, straight through a large smoke ring, which she wore like a spectral ruff for the seconds it took to disperse. 'Gran's bad enough, but *Granny*? Out of my shop at once, woman!'

Jilly came further in. Inger left the office.

'I imagine you've come for your book,' she said. Jilly went blank. 'The cookery tome you ordered last week...?'

'It's in already?'

'We're nothing if not efficient here.' Inger ducked below the counter for the book and held it up briefly for Jilly's inspection. 'Do the honours, will you, Midge?' She handed her the book. 'She wraps better than I do,' she told Jilly.

Jilly touched her hair with her fingertips in case a whisper of breeze had wheedled its way through the wall of heat outside and dared disturb a strand. 'I really came in for something else,' she said. 'Some-*one* else.'

'Oh?'

Pouncing on a neat pile of information leaflets with the sole intention, it seemed, of making a mess of them, Jilly elaborated.

'I was wondering if Midge would care to join us for lunch and spend some more time with Nat. And Henrietta, of course, though Henry's quite self-sufficient and independent for her age. She can always find ways of amusing herself.'

Midge had given her grandmother a fairly precise

account of her encounter with Nathaniel and received a pledge that she would not have to endure his company again. But here she was being asked to offer her up for further sacrifice. Could she refuse? Midge attempted telepathy:

Save me. Please. I'll do anything, just don't let her take me.

'He's driving you up the wall, isn't he?' Inger said to Jilly.

The information leaflets dropped from her friend's fingers. Her eyes were large and helpless. 'All the way to the ceiling.'

A lesser woman might have weakened at this and handed her granddaughter over screaming, but Inger proved, to Midge's immense gratitude, that she was made of sterner stuff.

'You have my sympathies, dear, but Midge has a prior engagement.' She swung a reassuring arm round her assistant's shoulders. 'We have to visit her incontinent Uncle Jim in a nursing home in Weymouth.'

'You've never mentioned an Uncle Jim in a nursing home,' Jilly said suspiciously.

Inger shook her head sadly. 'We don't talk about him.'

'Oh. Well perhaps they'll get together at the barbecue.'

Inger's fingers crushed Midge's shoulder. 'Barbecue?'

'You haven't forgotten my High Summer Barbie on Saturday?'

'Forgotten?' Inger said, rather too hastily. 'Of course we haven't forgotten. We were just saying how much we're looking forward to it. Weren't we, Midge?'

She dug her fingernails into the already damaged shoulder and shot its owner a lightning glance of dismay to show her true feelings about the barbecue. Midge made a high-pitched 'Mm!' sound. Those nails were sharp.

When Jilly had gone, Midge said: 'Uncle Jim in a nursing home?'

Inger grinned. 'Spur of the moment relative.'

'But what if she comes back and we're still here?'

The grin dissolved. 'Perhaps we'd better go out anyway.'

'What, shut the shop?'

'Oh, I couldn't do that, this is my busiest month.'

'Not so busy today,' Midge pointed out.

'It'll pick up this afternoon. Have to call in the reserves again. Once I track him down. I don't know where that man gets to half the time.'

'Where are we going?' Midge asked as they climbed into the Volvo after lunch.

'I told Jilly Weymouth,' Inger said, adjusting her sunglasses, 'so why not Weymouth? I think we'll give the nursing home a miss though, don't you, seeing as we're a bit short of incontinent Uncle Jims?'

She started the car, looked left and right, ignored the evidence of her own eyes, and flung it across the road so that the red sports car doing forty down the high street was forced to brake hard. The driver blasted her with his horn.

'Road hog!' Inger yelled into the rear-view mirror.

With a business to run, Inger left Steepridge far less often than she might have wished, so the crowded resort of Weymouth made a change for her too. 'We should take you out more often,' she said as they strolled through the town after parking the car. 'It's not fair on you, cooped up inside all day, specially in weather like this. Pity about all these people, though. People should be banned, along with traffic.'

That leisurely afternoon was the longest period of time Midge had ever spent alone in her grandmother's company outside the shop, and it turned out to be not such bad company at that. In her mid-sixties, slim, straight-backed, alert, Inger wasn't much less vivacious than she'd been in her twenties, or much less shapely. Men of all ages eyed her up in passing, and she revelled in it, quite blatantly, to Midge's occasional embarrassment and secret pride. A gran who turned men's heads: now wasn't *that* something? She must have driven them wild when she first walked into Dorset with Juby all those years ago. This afternoon she wore Roman-style sandals, a white cotton skirt (which became translucent when the sun was behind or in front of her), and a shirt of turquoise silk. No bra. Very *evidently* no bra. She'd drawn her hair back, fitted earrings that swung like golden nooses, and wore more bangles on her wrists than Midge even possessed. If I could look half that sexy at a third her age, she thought, I'd be well-pleased.

Inger would also have worn the hat she kept in the car had she not, just as they were setting out, slammed the boot on it and effectively sliced it in two. In need of a replacement she insisted on Midge having one as well, so they went into a seafront gift shop where Midge chose a broad-brimmed straw effort with ragged edges and Inger opted for a white mini sombrero with KISS ME SLOW on the front. When she saw herself in the mirror she laughed like a Norwegian drain. Midge covered her eyes.

It came as no surprise that Inger was a mine of information about Weymouth. She was a mine of information about many things, ascribing her wide-ranging knowledge of trivia to 'all those years sitting on my duff in the shop, reading anything that comes to hand while waiting for browsers.' Weymouth, as a subject, would not ordinarily have piqued Midge's interest in the slightest, but presented by Inger, with her lively delivery and her slight but unusual accent, even the dullest of facts sounded as if they stood a chance of being worth listening to any time now. Her history teacher would have had her stifling a yawn with: 'Henry VIII turned Weymouth harbour into a naval base'. Coming from Inger she actually found herself paying attention and thinking, 'Hey, must remember that.'

One of her fragments of enlightenment caused quite a laugh, if only for Midge. They were strolling along the Esplanade, having just bought cones of Mr Mario icecream, and Inger was telling Midge, who hadn't asked, how George III, sampling the waters here in the late seventeen hundreds, had become the first recorded English monarch to take a voluntary dip in the sea. 'A vastly stupid act that started the craze for sea bathing that's with us still,' she said. 'When you think that Georgie boy was completely off his twig, one can but wonder about the sanity of the hundreds of thousands of lemmings who follow his example every summer. I mean to say, just *look* at them!'

At 'just look at them' the hand holding the Mr Mario flew out to indicate the beach crowded with sunbathers, swimmers and paddlers. The cone remained in her grip, but the soft vanilla ice, expelled by the jerk of her arm, leapt in a high arc and came down on a shoulder of a deckchair attendant chatting with a group of senior citizens. The attendant looked from his book of tickets to the large white spreading epaulet just below his right ear. His mouth dropped open – not to sample a free Mr Mario – and his amazed eyes lifted slowly to an enormous seagull gliding innocently overhead.

They were sitting on a bench facing the sea when Midge, more to fill a rare moment of silence than anything else, asked Inger what she knew about Rouklye, to which she replied: 'As much as anyone who's lived in the vicinity for far too long. What do you want to know?'

She wasn't sure; admitted this.

'Rouklye was mentioned in the Domesday Book,' Inger said. 'You've heard of the Domesday Book?'

'Yes, we did it at school a couple of years ago.'

'Well, that was in 1086 – not when you did it, when it was written up. But even before that, long before, there was a Roman settlement in the valley, and evidence of Iron Age activity has been found there too.'

'I'm interested in this century,' said Midge.

'Oh, I can quote entire guidebooks on *this* century,' Inger said.

'Is there a short version?'

'There's always a short version. Try this. For hundreds of years Rouklye was a self-contained community going about its business away from the traumas and trials of history, and—'

'You sound like you're quoting.'

'I'm paraphrasing. Over time the village – along with much of the rest of the valley – underwent many changes of ownership, but it belonged to a single family for the last five centuries. The woods and meadows all about abounded with every kind of flora, the streams and ponds were well-stocked with— How am I doing?'

'Shorter?' Midge said.

'—with fish. During the first third of this century, much of the surrounding area was acquired by the Ministry of Defence for training purposes, and when the 1939 war came they saw their chance to get their mitts on the rest, and took it, in the most literal sense. Anything else?'

'No, that'll do.'

'And what's your opinion?'

'Opinion?'

'Of the rights and wrongs of government departments appropriating private property for their own ends.'

'I…' She shrugged.

'Oh, come on, Midge. Several hours in the company of Mr Bench, who makes no bones about where *he* stands, must have persuaded you onto one side of the fence or the other.'

'I didn't know there was a fence.'

'Didn't you? Well, there is. To this day, local opinion is *very* divided on the issue.'

A little later Inger spotted an amusement arcade across the road. 'What do you say we go over there,' she said, 'and squander some dosh on pointless games and rigged slot machines?'

'I haven't got any money,' Midge confessed.

From thin air Inger produced a crisp twenty pound note, which she stuffed into Midge's hand – 'What are you talking about, child?' – flipped her hat to a rakish angle, and marched to the curb, from where she stood glaring at the holiday traffic that streamed between her and the arcade. Midge joined her a second after she walked into the road, hand held high to inform the traffic rushing towards her at breakneck speed that it had better watch itself or it would answer to her. Brakes squealed. Mouths twisted in anger. Inger Bjølstad was in town.

FIFTEEN

Although Edwin cooked the meal that night and was at the table to eat with them, he kept his eyes on his plate throughout, said little, and gruffly excused himself the moment he was done instead of waiting for the others to finish and clearing away personally as usual. It was a relief when he left the room, but Inger rolled her eyes in irritation.

'This is crazy. And him a grown man with a bus pass.'

After they'd washed up – something else Edwin usually did – Inger, determined to 'put an end to this nonsense', sent Midge down the garden on a particular errand. She had never seen her grandfather in a really bad mood before, so she approached his shed rather timidly. The notice on the ominously closed door did nothing to improve her confidence.

> **PRIVATE!**
> NO HAWKERS
> NO JEHOVAH'S WITNESSES
> NO NORWEGIANS

The Pottering Shed was Edwin Underwood's bolt-hole; the place he went to when he wanted to be in his own world rather than someone else's.* One of the things he did to occupy himself here was work on small-scale construction kits. In the early days these kits had provided more frustration than satisfaction, as few of the models he'd attempted had ended up bearing more than a passing resemblance to the pictures on the boxes. But then, a while ago, he'd come up with a brilliant solution: only buy kits marked 'For 10 and Under'. As a result the Pottering Shed was now home to a cornucopia of miniature planes, spaceships, boats, automobiles and

---

* The shed had been delivered in kit form five years ago and had remained unconstructed for some eighteen months while Edwin puzzled over the assembly instructions in Italian, German, French and English, and stared at all the little polythene bags of screws, washers and other things that didn't generally play a very important role in his life. Occasionally he hoisted a panel of wood to try and imagine how the shed would look when built, but that was as far as he got until Fred Gittens, a neighbour whose wife had recently left him (also leaving him with time on his hands), joined him in the instruction-solving. Between them they decided what should go where, and erected the shed. The day they finished this monumental task they went over to The Ferryman to celebrate. By the time they returned from the celebratory drink the shed had collapsed, so they went back to The Ferryman to drown their sorrows. The shed might have remained in this forlorn state until it rotted if not for Fred's younger brother Tom. Tom Gittens, a builder by trade, didn't need instructions in any language. He assembled the shed almost single-handedly in one hour thirty-five minutes. This time it did not fall down.

castles. Some of them were even painted, but he'd given this up when he discovered that painting was another skill he had yet to acquire.

The Pottering Shed was also where Edwin organised his four stamp albums (90% of whose stamps came from a subscription firm in Somerset) and kept his little portable television. He had told no one about his TV because he didn't want it getting back to Inger, whose dislike of the medium was so extreme that even in his sanctuary he kept the sound well down for fear her Nordic antennae would pick it up from the house. To cut the risk of her barging in and spotting the set, he kept the door locked at all times, when he was in the shed and when he was not. What he didn't know was that one evening a few weeks ago, anxious to get to The Ferryman for a swift half before closing, he'd bungled the locking process and the door had swung open a couple of inches as he scuttled past Inger on her way to fetch the washing from the line. Inger had never found the shed open before, and, being a naturally curious person, had not gone out of her way to resist the urge to look inside this one time. She had not mentioned what she saw there, to Edwin or anyone else. For now, the knowing was sufficient.

When he heard a nervous little tap on the door,

Edwin tumbled out of the lumpy old armchair he'd bought for a tenner at an auction in Church Knowle, threw himself headlong at the TV, and flicked off the sentimental American sitcom he'd not been laughing at.

'Who is it?'

'Me. Midge.'

He covered the set with a blanket he kept handy for thoughtless interruptions, unlocked the door, and peered out with one eye to check that it was indeed Midge and not some impersonator trying to fool him.

'Gran thought you might like a cup of tea.'

He eyed the white cup and saucer in her hand. 'I have my own kettle, she knows that.'

'I'll take it back if you like,' Midge said, hoping he'd agree so she could make a swift departure. As it was she who'd gone to Rouklye with Juby, she assumed that his anger must, in part, be aimed at her, which made her uncomfortable in his presence. But:

'No. Might as well have it as you've taken the trouble.'

He opened the door a bit more and extended his hand for the cup and saucer.

'She sent this too.' Midge held out an envelope.

'What is it, the bill?'

'She didn't say.' He took the envelope in his other hand, even more suspicious of it than the tea, turned it over, sniffed it, held it up to the light. 'She said to tell you to read it while I'm here.'

'She wants a written reply?'

'I don't know.'

'Hm! Well – you'd better come in.'

Having no idea what an honour was being bestowed upon her, she entered. The shed was a comfortable mess, just the way Edwin liked it, and smelt of wood and glue and enclosed man. The white roller blinds pulled down over the windows were designed to let in the light but not be seen through. It was very warm in there in spite of the small electric fan. The fan was set on 'rotate', which meant that it swept the interior, left to right, right to left, fanning each part in turn. Every time it came back to the middle, where the door was, Midge's hair stood on end. Edwin, with his wispy little side bits, had no such problem.

"Scuse the mess.'

'This is nothing, you should see my room at home.' Her room at home wasn't anything like as bad as this, but it seemed the thing to say.

'Park your hind-quarters.'

She looked for somewhere to sit. The choice was either the lumpy old armchair or the high stool at the workbench. The workbench contained his electric kettle, several mugs long overdue for a wash, a plate of old sandwich crusts, a motley assortment of unpainted models, and the secret TV under the blanket. She opted for the stool. Edwin set down the cup and saucer and opened the envelope. Reading Inger's note, he was soon frowning.

'Is there an answer?' Midge asked.

'Oh, there's an answer all right,' he snarled as he finished reading. 'But I think I'll deliver it personally. Stay here!' He yanked the door back and charged out, leaving it swinging.

She slipped off the stool, and, through the vertical slit between the hinges, watched him stalk up the path. Inger had positioned herself at the kitchen window in anticipation of just such a response, and as he approached she leaned forward, daring him to confront her. Edwin's step faltered. He knew that look. It said 'Mess with me, Underwood, and you're a carcass.' For almost half-a-minute the two stood glaring at one another through the glass, then Edwin squared his shoulders, held the note up, and ripped it to small pieces, which he flicked defiantly into the air. Finally, he whirled about and stormed back up the path.

Midge rushed to the stool. Her hand shook a little as she reached for something to pretend to be examining.

She picked up a small model helicopter. One of the rotor blades immediately fell off.

If she'd glanced Edwin's way on his return she would have seen his whole demeanour change radically and the bright light of rebellion fade from his eye. His hands fell limply to his sides as he walked to his chair, for once living, rather than playing, the part of Poor Little Downtrodden Man. She heard the creak of the armchair as he sat, and waited, fingers tightly laced to prevent their reaching out and destroying anything else.

'I've been ordered by she-who-must-be-obeyed,' Edwin said quietly to her back, 'to tell you why I get so uptight about Juby and Rouklye.'

It was something that had really got under his skin over the years and scratched away at him until it was a full-blown weeping sore. He might not have mentioned it at all if Inger's note hadn't informed him that if he didn't clear the air this very evening ('so the girl can stop thinking it's her fault') he could kiss goodbye to a quiet life. It wasn't easy finding the words, though, and all Midge could hear while he struggled to locate a few was such a silence that she began to wonder if he was all right. In the end she turned round to see. No, he hadn't quietly died, he was just sitting there, deep in his chair, looking very small and ineffectual. The look of him, from her elevated position on the high stool, fortified her nerve.

'Juby and Rouklye?'

It must have been the nudge he needed, because he scowled anew and jerked forward in his chair, shoulders hunched.

'Juby and Rouklye!' It was so very nearly a roar that it took all of her nerve not to run to the door. 'I'll tell you about Juby and Rouklye!' Edwin said, a little less vehemently, but not much. 'Every August, rain, hail or shine, that man tootles over from Germany in his old banger to tell anyone who'll lend him an ear what life used to be like in his perfect English village. Then, having filled a whole new batch of gullible heads with his nonsense, he shoves off home again, mission accomplished. It makes me mad at the best of times, but now he's filling *your* head with it, and it boils my blood!'

Midge stared. Could it really be that two elderly men who were boys together in the same village had fallen out because they disagreed about what it had been like *living* there? How idiotic. How ludicrous. How unbelievably pathetic.

Edwin caught her incredulity, suspected the cause, and wagged his head in embarrassment. He'd always known this thing between him and Juby wasn't terribly rational, but before Midge's astonished stare he felt quite foolish. When next he spoke he went out of his way to sound more reasonable.

'All I'm saying, Midge, is that if you want to know what it was like in Rouklye I'm the one to ask, not Juby. To hear him, Rouklye was heaven on earth. Not a strand of honeysuckle out of place, sun always shining, workers singing happily in the fields, the full sepia scenario. Bet he hasn't mentioned the privations.'

'Privations?'

'Having to walk to the pump for water in all weathers and carry it home in buckets. Scavenging in the woods for fuel. Huddling round smoky fires by sputtering lamplight, bored witless because there was bugger all to do. We didn't even have a radio. No electricity, see. They had electricity up at the big house, but not in the village. No flush toilets either. Let me tell you, my recent dive into old Crapper's masterpiece might not have made my day, but when it's working it's a hell of an advance on the stinking hole in the ground we had to use back then – and empty every few days with our own fair hands.'

He paused, perhaps expecting questions. None came. Not being used to this side of him, the best Midge could do, for the moment, was sit tight and hear him out.

So he continued. 'Listen to the Jubys of this world and you'll come away believing that if the Army hadn't taken over the valley everything would be exactly the same as he imagines it was before, only with a symphonic soundtrack. Well it wouldn't, by a long chalk. This isn't the Middle Ages. Things don't stand still for centuries any more. There'd be roads with double yellow lines, new houses with white plastic doors, satellite dishes wherever you looked, a kebab joint or a chippy, supermarket windows full of gaudy stickers. The rectory cottages would've been converted into "desirable residences", there'd be Porsches in Post Office Row, the church would have been taken over by a firm of solicitors with a string of unbelievable names, and as for the old schoolhouse, my guess is it would be either a chic little restaurant or an organic tea shop with wholemeal scones and 26 varieties of herbal tea.'

He was on his hobby horse, and cantering, eyes bright with the will to spill the true beans.

'There'd be a pub too. There never was a pub in Rouklye, just some old boy brewing ale in his parlour for a few pennies. Nowadays there'd be this yellow brick monstrosity – *The Cat and the Idyll* or somesuch – for the tourists to sit outside on summer evenings tossing crisp packets over their shoulders before driving back to their rented caravans on the cliff. And every Saturday night a gang of tanked-up hooligans from some nearby council estate would be bellowing at the top of their voices and kicking lager cans round the oh-so-nicely sculptured village green, which would probably have a graffiti-covered statue of the Thatcher woman wielding a scroll. There wasn't some sort of preserving spell on the place, Midge. Rouklye wasn't excused by royal decree from time's march. The fact that it was just another common-or-garden village seems to have been forgotten by many and completely overlooked by those who came after. Now that it's reduced to rubble people can amble around picturing it as they like to think it was; rebuild it in their minds as a lost haven of tranquillity, unchanged and unchanging, roses round every door and...' He drew a long breath at last. 'Well, you probably get my drift.'

'If you feel like that about it,' Midge said, 'why do you keep all those old photos?'

He frowned. 'Old photos?'

'The ones on the walls of my room.'

'Oh, those. My mother's. Mum was a bit of a photographer, travelled a lot in her youth, took photos in places I can't even find on the map. When the war came she set about photographing Rouklye and its environs in case it was bombed. It wasn't bombed, though it might as well have been, given the end result. I framed her Rouklye prints after she died, put them in the spare room – as a tribute to her as much as anything – along with those rocks of hers.'

'The rocks were hers too?'

'Yes. She was a geologist by profession.'

It hadn't so much as crossed her mind that the pictures could have been taken by her great-grandmother; that the rocks might have been hers either. She was amazed at her lack of perception. The chess set was hers, she'd known that, and the photos belonged more to her generation than Edwin's...

'Did your mother live here then?' she asked. 'In this house?'

A short laugh. 'No. Never. Not even in Dorset after the evacuation. I was already in digs in Wareham by then, and she went to stay with her brother in Huntingdonshire till the war ended. Then she was off. Hardly saw or heard from her for years on end. She was in her late seventies when she was killed.'

Midge's mouth went dry. *'Killed!'*

'In Mombasa. The president of Kenya had just died and a bunch of students decided to celebrate by nicking a jeep. A security officer took a pot-shot at them, missed the driver, hit my mother in the eye. The left one, I think. Died instantly, they said.'

'No one ever told me about this,' she said in horror.

'Happened before your mum was born. I told her the story when she was about your age, year or two younger maybe, but she shrugged it off. Malena was always more interested in the living, the present day.'

'Like Dad.'

'Yeah, like your dad. Peas in a pod, those two.'

'What was your mother doing in…where was it?'

'Mombasa. Not a clue. Never found out. She was always off somewhere in the world. Liked to be where things were buzzing, or it felt like a buzz was imminent. That didn't include England most of the time. I don't take after her. Real stay-at-home, me, always was.'*

'Tell me more about growing up in Rouklye,' Midge said.

He eyed her suspiciously. 'Why? To compare my version with Juby's?'

She wriggled uncomfortably. He wasn't far wrong. Nevertheless, he obliged.

'For Juby,' he said, 'there was nowhere like Rouklye. Nor me, till I hit my teens. Nothing to compare it with, you see. There wasn't much in the way of transport then,

---

* For more about Larissa Underwood at her brother's house in the 1940s, the life she saved there and the future history she changed, see *Small Eternities*, Book 2 of *The Aldous Lexicon* trilogy.

so we rarely left the valley. We played and wandered for miles without fear, hunted rabbit, pheasant, fished more or less wherever we wanted, raided orchards...' He sat back in his chair. 'Sounds good, doesn't it? And it was, if you were young, innocent, kept your nose clean. We had a lot more freedom than today's kids, that's for sure. But it was an illusory freedom. Most of the valley was owned by the family up at the big house: the Flemings. They weren't a bad lot for their class, but you were never in much doubt where you stood in life's pecking order. Even in church they had their own pews away from us peasants. The supreme defender of the hierarchy principle was the Rector. Nasty type, full of himself, boomed the scriptures from the pulpit on Sunday and off-duty strutted about in plus-fours scowling at youngsters and working people. He carried a tasselled leather dog whip and didn't hesitate to use it – not always on dogs. Lashed me with it once for smirking as he passed. When Mum saw the marks she went after him, cracked him across the head with a broom handle and asked him how he liked it. He never touched me again.'

'Good for her,' said Midge.

'Yeah. The old dear had her moments. But this thing about knowing your place. When we boys saw the squire sweeping the countryside with his binoculars, we thought he was keeping an eye on us to make sure we weren't up to no good. It was years before we found out that he was a keen bird-watcher and probably not bothered about us at all, but that wasn't the point. The *point* was that it was his land and he had the right to tick us off, march us home, even demand that we were given a good hiding if it suited him. As we got older that started to get to some of us. A couple of my mates left the village when they were old enough, got jobs outside, and when I was fourteen I followed their lead. *Then* I felt free, even though I had to mind my ps and qs with my boss and work longer hours than anyone should have to for such a pittance.'

Midge caught a movement outside, a shadow crossing one of the opaque white blinds. A movement and a shadow which Edwin, caught up in his lecture, missed.

'I wasn't in Rouklye when the order to quit came. Most people left without fuss, and it didn't take them long to realise that there was a lot to be said for the mod cons they hadn't had before. Some profited in other ways too. There were more soldiers about, and they spent well – particularly the yanks when they were here in the early days – and a few of them started families with local lasses. Before you knew it, the military had become part of the community, and…'

Another movement outside, which, this time, he noticed. A small creak of something touching wood: a hand perhaps, or an ear. Edwin put a finger to his lips, eased himself out of his chair, and crept (Tom-and-Jerrylike) to the door. When he gave it a thump with the side of his fist, there was a small yelp on the other side, and footsteps scurrying away.

He returned to his chair, settled back, legs stretched out before him. 'Where was I?'

'Some people preferred life outside Rouklye.'

'Yes. Right. But Juby wasn't one of them. For him, nowhere else could touch Rouklye. There was a reason for that, of course. I mean he wasn't really *one* of us.'

He gave her the kind of look that seeks to share an amused confidence about the person under discussion; a confidence Midge found herself unwilling to share. Mildly indignant on Juby's behalf, she said: 'Why should he be one of you? What's so wrong with being an individual and liking the place you were born and grew up in?'

Edwin's eyebrows rose until they weren't far short of where his hairline had been when he was twenty-five.

'What the hell's the old twit been telling you now?'

'He just tells me what it was like there as he remembers it. He doesn't make out that it was all perfect the way you think he does. He has some good memories, that's all.'

The eyebrows returned to their usual level as he pondered her words. After a while, he said: 'You know, I think...'

'What do you think?' Midge asked when he left the rest hanging.

He drew his legs in and levered himself out of the chair. Then he squared his shoulders and adjusted his feet in such a way that she expected him to embark on one of his impressions: of a penguin perhaps. But he did not do a penguin, he did an Edwin Underwood, strolling in a wholly ordinary way to the workbench, where he leant on his elbows next to her, looking intently at the broken helicopter.

'I think we should see what can be done about this.'

SIXTEEN

More relaxed in Inger's company now that she'd spent time with her away from Edwin, Juby and Steepridge, Midge worked happily in the shop the morning after the trip to Weymouth. She even smiled more, and was more confident when dealing with customers. But the afternoon was quiet, and Inger insisted that she spend some of it in the garden, 'where the sun is', reading a collection of stories that she personally recommended. Sitting under a sycamore, in a rather creaky old deckchair, Midge at first enjoyed her garden exile – the stories, too, to her surprise – but grew restless after a couple of hours and went to her room hoping to find something to do there. In the event, all that she did was lie on her bed and doze, from which she woke feeling that the day had been wasted.

But in the evening something extraordinary happened. A something all the more extraordinary for its proximity to Edwin's rant about Juby and Rouklye. It started with a light knock on the kitchen door, which Edwin answered. There followed a brief exchange, at the conclusion of which he brought Juby in, waving a bottle of Scotch. What they talked about Midge couldn't have said afterwards, but it wasn't dull talk and she didn't feel in any way excluded from it or by it. Her age and limited experience of life made some difference, of course, but to her more than the others, it seemed. Juby and her grandparents were quite strong personalities while she – by her own estimation – was a shallow, colourless creature with few opinions of value. But she tried to look bright and nod in all the right places, offer contributions when invited, and they seemed to welcome this, as though they genuinely valued her input. At a certain point during the evening she came to the conclusion that she really liked these people, all three of them, different as they were from one another. She realised something else too. That they liked her. In their assembled company she felt like a fourth member of a charmed quartet. A sort of fourth rook. Now there was a thought.

As he was leaving, Juby offered his hand to Edwin and Edwin shook it. Juby nodded, just once, and

Edwin nodded once in return, a pair of identical question-and-answer gestures that said 'All right?' and 'All right,' but spoke volumes.

'Can't remember when I last saw them so chummy,' Inger whispered to Midge. 'Must be your influence.'

'Mine? I haven't done anything.'

Her grandmother gave her shoulders a squeeze, but added nothing.

Up in her room, in the third letter she planned to post in a few days' time, Midge told Nessa about the evening. 'I'M AN INFLUENCE!', she crowed. It was late, so it was not a long letter, but she envied her friend all the news she would read on her return and looked forward to filling in the gaps when she too was back home. So often when they were together she sat or walked quietly within the arc of Nessa's easy charm while hearing of this or that discovery, insight, passing fancy. Ness would inevitably have a great deal to tell her about her holiday in Pembrokeshire, but for once, surely, it would be she, Midge, who would have the really fascinating tale to tell. Whatever she'd experienced in Wales, Ness would have met no one like Juby Bench, been nowhere as odd as Rouklye, and certainly not experienced a phenomenon like the almost-there boy. She considered her accumulating news. What if nothing else happened and she'd already put the best bits in the letters?

If that were the case, there'd be nothing much to add when she and Nessa met. Maybe she should hold back on future info; merely hint that stuff was happening. Yes. That way she stood a chance of keeping her friend enthralled while she talked. What a reversal *that* would be!

The sun lay like a golden carpet all along the street. It was just after lunch and she was outside, tidying the rack of second-hand books that Inger put there every day to attract passers-by. A reflection caught her eye in the window: Juby, stooping out of the doorway of The Ferryman. She saw him glance her way, hesitate, then cross the road, his great black jacket flapping round him as though about to bear him up, up and away.

'Another hott'un, Evy.'

She half turned. He looked tired, all lines and furrows, even more than at breakfast the other morning.

'Yeah. Late today, aren't you?'

'Yeah. Couldn't seem to get the old bones off the mattress.'

'Too much of that whisky,' she said.

'Not enough, more like.' He bent down to inspect the rack. 'Still using you as slave-labour, is she?'

'I'm just passing the time. Trish is here, so I'm not really needed.'

'Trish?'

'She comes in to help out two days a week.'

'Even though you're here?'

'It's a regular arrangement. Going to Rouklye again?'

'Yes. Just off.'

She watched him fingering the spines, tried to imagine him at sixteen, when he must have looked so like the almost-there boy. Could the boy *be* him? she wondered. The ghost of Juby as a lad? Could you have a ghost of someone who wasn't dead, a spectre of them at an earlier point in their life? If so, was he trying to communicate with her from the past for some reason? Well, next time she'd be looking out for him, ready for him. But the only place she'd seen him so far – perhaps the only place he *could* be seen – was…

'I could go with you again,' she said.

Bent over from the waist, Juby continued to tug books out and shove them back as though he hadn't heard her.

'We needn't rush about,' she added hopefully.

'You've seen all there is,' he muttered.

'I don't mind seeing it again.'

He straightened up; squinted down at her.

'What is all this?'

'All what?'

'The sudden interest in Rouklye.'

She rushed a false confession. 'Just thought you might like the company. But if you don't, fine, I can find things to do here.'

He explored her face thoughtfully, for seconds that felt like minutes to her, before: 'You know, there's something about you that I can't quite put my finger on.'

Self-conscious enough without those penetrating eyes finding further fault, it took a supreme effort for her not to look away.

'Like what?' she said, not sure she wanted to know.

'As I said, I can't put my finger on it. You'll have to get permission.'

'Permission?'

'To go with me.'

'It's all right, I'll stay here. I said.'

'You don't want to come then?'

'It's not important.'

'It might be.'

'Eh?'

'Why don't you go and ask?'

'Ask who what?'

'Edwin. For his blessing.'

'I'll ask Gran.'

'No,' Juby said. 'Edwin this time.'

'Why his?'

'Because that's the way it has to be.'

He told her he would wait in the car park of The Ferryman for fifteen minutes. If she wasn't there by the end of that time he would go without her. He crossed the street and Midge went into the shop. Trish was sorting books and Inger was flicking through publishers' catalogues.

'Juby says I can go to Rouklye with him again if it's all right,' she said.

Inger tutted irritably. 'I wish you wouldn't. Look at the upset it causes. You'll have to ask Edwin.'

'I was going to. Where is he?'

'That stupid hidey-hole of his.'

She hurried down the garden and pressed an ear to the door of the Pottering Shed. The distant sound of a muted cricket commentary, the thwack of leather on willow, the roar of a crowd constrained by the small speakers of his portable television turned low. She knew about the TV. Edwin, finger to lips, had revealed it to her towards the end of her previous visit. She knocked. A startled crash from inside, then the cricket commentary was silenced.

'Who's there? Friend or Viking?'

'Midge.'

The door opened to reveal an eye and half a nose.

The eye explored the space around her, saw that she was alone, and the door opened a fraction more to make room for a second eye and the rest of the nose.

'Want to come in?'

'No, I just have to ask if...'

She hesitated, worried that he would hit the roof.

'Talk to me, Midge, talk to me, the West Indies are beating the bails off England in here.'

'Promise you won't be annoyed.'

'Me, annoyed? When am I ever annoyed?'

'When I go to Rouklye with Juby.'

Edwin's brows knitted together in the small space provided.

'What the heck's so fascinating about a bunch of old ruins?'

'I won't if you don't want me to,' she said.

'Are you asking my leave?'

'He says I must.'

Amazement filled the eyes in the doorway. 'He told you to ask *me*?' She nodded. 'Well whaddayaknow.'

'It'll be all right,' she said. 'Really. And...'

'And what?'

'It is only a point of view.'

Edwin gave a hoot of laughter; then: 'If I say yes, one favour in return.'

'What's that?'

'Take it all with a very large pinch of salt.'

'That's it?' she said.

'That's it.'

He shut the door without waiting for her agreement, and once again Midge accompanied Juby to Rouklye – with no idea that she would learn something today that would make this August as memorable as any in her entire life, past or future.

SEVENTEEN

After a shaky start it was turning into the kind of summer
people dream about, dress down for, and complain about
if it lasts for more than a few days. In parts of the
country water companies were threatening to ration
supplies, in Yorkshire and Somerset hosepipe bans were
already in force, and beaches were packed solid with
brown and red bodies. Visitors to Rouklye who fancied
a spot of sea air had to trek out to Crowbarrow on foot,
but there, though they could sprawl on the sand and
shingle and dip their toes in the water, they could not,
as they might elsewhere, rent deckchairs and
powerboats, or buy ice creams and fizzy drinks, buckets
and spades. This was Ministry of Defence property, after
all, not a holiday resort.

There were workmen in Post Office Row today. Two paint-flecked ladders leant against the inner walls of one of the cottages as the men filled gaps in brick- and stonework. Juby stood watching them for a minute, then went next door. Midge did not follow him. She no longer felt obliged to go everywhere he did, and doubted that he expected her to. Not having known these buildings when they were whole and in daily use she could not share his nostalgia for them, but it was curious: each time she came here she was a bit more intrigued by the place and the people who'd lived here. She had no trouble taking Edwin's advice about Juby's view of the old days in Rouklye, but, charmed by that view, she saw no reason to discard it completely.

There was something else too: the voices, which seemed clearer with each visit. There seemed to be more of them each time as well. She could hear them now, within the shell of the old post office, though when she went in they seemed to retreat a little, as if stepping back into their true realm of residency. She listened hard, wished she could make out what they said, but a clarity-denying barrier stood between her and the voices. There was nothing scary about them. They worried her no more than the occasional movement at the corner of her eye worried her.

When Juby again led the way down to his former house, Midge discovered that his purpose was no longer merely to gaze and remember. 'Made some headway yesterday,' he told her, fishing a pair of secateurs from his trouser pocket. 'Make a bit more today, and tomorrow, with any luck, I'll be through.'

'You're trying to get to the house?' she said in alarm.

'Sssh, voice down, trees are probably bugged. Keep a look-out.'

He plunged into the undergrowth, leaving her a startled guard at the perimeter.

'But the signs,' she hissed. 'They say it's unsafe.'

'Whole world's unsafe,' Juby grunted. 'Take note of every sign and you never do a damn thing. Eyes peeled now.'

Peeled eyes darting all over the place, she did her best not to look like a partner-in-crime, pretending merely to have paused to admire the towering weeds. To mask the clip-clip-clip of the secateurs, she began whistling a catchy little song she disliked, though the odd passer-by still glanced curiously at her. After some minutes of this she got fed up and, choosing her moment, went in after Juby. Something sharp tore her arm, introducing a quick red line to the flesh. She saw scratches on Juby's arms too, but, intent on his task, he seemed unaware of them. He was indeed closer to the house than the last time she'd come here with him, but today's efforts did not take him all the way as he'd hoped, the secateurs proving inadequate against heavy-duty barbed-wire.

'Fool!' he growled. 'Has to be tomorrow now,' and added, just under his breath: 'Given the time.'

Rouklye church was the only building Juby had shown no inclination to visit while she was with him, but today, as he loitered in the shade of the King's oak, Midge noticed him inching casually towards the steps as though the movement were beyond his control or notice. Faintly amused by this, she seized the initiative, bounded up them, and at the top, in the unusual position of being taller than Juby Bench, said: 'Coming?'

He frowned up at her. 'Where?'

'The church.'

'The church? Me?'

'Yes, let's take a look.'

He made a disapproving sound deep in his throat, but when she turned away he took the first step up, then the next, and the next, slowly, grudgingly, and before long stood a yard or so from her, at the top.

Elsewhere the grass was browned and stunted from weeks of inexorable sunshine and a complete absence of rain, but up here the turf was as green as could be. Heavily-corroded iron crosses were dotted among headstones so immaculate that they might have been there no time at all, though the dates chiselled into them belied this.

'They send squaddies to scrub them with wire brushes,' Juby said. 'Water the grass too. Mustn't let the public think they've let the *church* go, whatever else.'

'Is it just this one you don't like,' she asked, 'or all churches?'

He scowled. 'Wouldn't catch me dead in any one of 'em. Pagan ritual dolled up to look respectable. Superstitious claptrap, start to finish.'

'I wouldn't mind a look inside.'

'Up to you. Free country. Was once anyway.'

On the way to the church, Midge glanced with fleeting interest at two headstones, but stopped in something very like shock at a third.

WILLIAM LEONARD BROOKER
Beloved Son of Rouklye
Born Here 1904, Mourned Here 1921

The grave of Billy Brooker. She hadn't given Billy a thought for two days, but this latest evidence of his erstwhile existence hit her hard. She'd seen a photo of him as a boy of about eight, seen the last remnants of the house in which he might have uttered his first cry and been laid out just seventeen years later, and now she stood at his final resting place. Wondering if the boy had ever left this valley in that short lifetime, she moved on.

The heavy oak door of the church stood ajar. She slipped inside, to a world where shadows clung to some walls, and sunlight, streaming through coloured glass, splashed others and brought a rainbow glow to the mellow wood of pews and lecterns. A few people wandered about, talking in hushed voices. A young couple in shorts and canvas shoes flipped reverently through an enormous leather-bound bible with faded gold tooling. Three elderly ladies selected picture postcards from a revolving rack that squealed with every turn, and dipped into their purses for coins to drop in the 'honesty box'. A notice behind the rack told how some of the original stained glass had been smashed after the evacuation (whether by intent or accident was not made clear) and other panels removed for preservation elsewhere, along with the three-sided Jacobean pulpit and a mighty old pipe-organ that had stood in the chancel. Replacement furniture and artefacts had been brought in since the church was restored and reopened to the public – as a curiosity, not for worship or any of the other traditional purposes.

Midge gazed about her. Clean and cared-for as it now was, the place lacked everything it must once have had, not least that musty, leathery, waxy smell of accumulated centuries. Abandoned for decades, then done up to be offered to the public as a perfect exhibit among ruins, it felt all wrong. About to leave – and gladly – she was attracted to an array of display boards fixed to the wall to one side of the door. They contained black-and-white photographs, printed documents, notes and hand-written letters, all of them in some way relevant to the Rouklye Valley of the years before the act that had so swiftly terminated its life and long history. She noticed two small posters advertising auctions of farm equipment, tools, utensils, furniture and livestock. Both were held in December 1943, one on the 9th, the other on the 14th, just days before the evacuation.

She was drawn to a set of prints of Crowbarrow and some of the people who'd lived there. In one, dated 1936, a bunch of fishermen were busy sorting a heavy mackerel catch on the beach. They might not all have been Millers, but she knew, now, that some probably were – and that she was almost certainly related to them.

In other pictures in this group, individuals were named. She recognised those of some of the Millers listed by Juby as they approached Crowbarrow, but one name she was sure he hadn't mentioned caught her eye. It belonged to a narrow-shouldered woman in a long apron who sat outside a cottage repairing a fishing basket. Her name: Midgie Miller.

One of the smaller displays was devoted to the Brooker family, with a photo of Billy himself as the centrepiece. He looked sixteen or seventeen, a graceless lad with a pleasant if not terribly bright face, holding a pail of milk in each hand. His mother and father smiled out of another picture, presumably also taken before the boy's death, and in a third and fourth three young women, their daughters, May, Rosie and Sarah, tried to look attractive for the camera. Saddened to have met Billy's family on the shadowed wall of the church after reading his epitaph in the brilliant light outside, Midge turned away, and in so doing saw two faces that were immediately both familiar and strange: Edwin and Juby in their early teens, the one squat and beaming, the other lanky and fidgety. They stood with a tall confident-looking woman with untidy hair who stared intently as if daring the photographer to include her in such nonsense. The caption read:

'Miss LM Underwood with son Edward and friend Joey'. Edward and Joey. She wondered how many other names the organisers had got wrong as she peered first at the boys' young faces, then at that of the great-grandmother who had ended her days so far from here, so horribly.

Leaving the exhibits, Midge caught a glimpse of something attached to the back of the door. She looked closer, at a typewritten sheet of paper. She found out later that it was a photocopy of a notice that had been pinned to the door by some of the villagers as they were leaving their homes that December of 1943.

> Please treat the church and houses with care.
> We have given up our homes, where many of us
> have lived for generations, to help win the war
> and keep men free. We shall return one day and
> thank you for treating the village kindly.

She found Juby still in the churchyard, but no nearer the church, standing in a brilliant arc of sunshine between the dappled shadows of overhanging boughs, well away from the nearest crosses and headstones. As she approached, he said, without looking up:

'This is the place.'

'Place for what?'

'Where I want to lie.' He stamped a sandal lightly on

the grass. 'Good view of what's left. Not that I'll be sitting up and looking.'

As he raised his eyes from the bright clipped grass, the light caught them in such a way that from where she stood it was like looking through his skull, to the clear sky behind him.

'Are we friends, would you say, Evy?'

It was as unexpected as any question could be. Friends? With him? Friends were people your own age who you could relax with, not weird old men who hung around ruins and hated authority and churches. And she'd only met him a few days ago. How could you be friends with someone that ancient who you hardly knew? But there was only one answer that could be given to such a direct question, with such eyes upon you.

'I... I think so.'

'Good. Cos I need to tell you something and I'd rather tell it to a friend.'

She waited, wondering.

'Back in January,' Juby said, 'I went to the quack's. Hadn't been feeling right for a while. Chest pains, palpitations, giddy spells. He did some tests and when the results came back he called me in. Told me I had six months.'

'Six months?' she said. 'What for?' And immediately realised her foolishness.

'Six months maximum. Be lucky to see July, he said.'

'July? But it's...'

'August, yeah. So I'm lucky after all. Or stubborn. Had to hang on till they opened up for the month. Nearly didn't make it. I was a bit poorly, but I made myself get up, drove hell for leather till I was within sight of the hills. Perked up no end then. Coming home does that to a fella.'

It was probably the most appalling news she'd ever heard first-hand – even worse than hearing that her great-grandmother had been killed by a stray bullet in Africa. That had happened so long ago, to someone she'd never known, but this, here, right now, Juby Bench...

'Now you know why I've not been too keen on you accompanying me,' he went on. 'It could happen any time, any minute, no predicting except it'll be soon. That's why I'm in Rouklye every day. Don't want to die in the car, or my bed, or at the bar of The Ferryman.'

'You mean you want to die in *Rouklye?*' she said. 'But you can't!'

'I can't die?'

'Can't die here.'

'There's nowhere else I'd rather,' he said with a faint smile.

'What about the other day? That cliff we climbed.

I thought it was a bit of a strain for you, but…' She puffed her cheeks out in astonished dismay.

His smile dissolved. 'I shouldn't have done that with you there. I just wanted to walk up there one last time. Day after day, I look on everything I do and see here as for the last time. Very soon it will be.'

'What about your family in Germany? Shouldn't you be with them?'

'What, when I turn up my toes?' A curt shake of the head. 'I don't want an audience. I've said my goodbyes there.'

'Oh, they know then?'

'No, I just said goodbye – with special care, so they'll remember afterwards. You're the only one I've told.'

'But why *me*?' she said. 'Why not Gran?'

'Why you? Because you're like me.'

'Like you?'

'You feel for this place. And you hear things.'

'Hear things?'

'Footsteps?' he prompted. 'Whispers? Chatter? The odd little laugh?'

She took a breath. 'You mean you hear them too?'

'Sometimes. Not much this trip, but sometimes.'

'And the other day? On the way to Crowbarrow?'

'I heard nothing then. But I didn't doubt that you did.'

'Why do you believe that I hear these things?'

'The way you look sometimes,' he said. 'A little smile every so often at nothing. That's why I say you're like me. I doubt that many others hear. Rare birds, you and me, Evy. Rare birds.'

Unflattered, she turned her head; gazed past the schoolhouse to the woods in which the ruins of his house and several others stood. 'So there are ghosts here,' she murmured.

'Ghosts?' he said. 'Where'd you get that from?'

She looked back at him. 'What else would they be?'

'How about a small part of those that used to live here?'

'Eh?'

'Just the ones that hated to leave. Some might still be alive elsewhere, old folk in their twilight years, no inkling that a part of them – spirit, soul, whatever you want to call it – hangs about here still, in a quiet sort of way.'

It was an attractive notion. 'It would explain the boy,' she said.

'Boy? What boy?'

'He could be you as you were the day you left. The you that didn't want to go. He must be about the age you were then.'

'Are you telling me,' Juby said slowly, 'that you've seen *me* here – as a lad?'

'He has to be you. No one else could look like that. No offence.'

He was frankly amazed. 'I *never* see people. Never have. Just get the sense of them.' But then he laughed, with real, untrammelled amusement. 'A young me! Wooh! And you see me? Clearly?'

'Clear as day. Not often, but...' She stopped. There was more pressing business. 'Can we get back to the other thing?'

'Other thing?'

'You, and what's going to happen.'

The gravity of his situation flooded back. 'You mustn't tell anyone about it. No one, even Inger. I don't want people being careful what they say around me, or feeling sorry for me. I'm only telling you because I want you to do something for me.'

Both mystified and unnerved by this, she said: 'What could I do?'

'I want you to see that they put me here.' He tapped his foot on his chosen plot. '*Right* here. I want no service, mind. No prayers or hymns or what-have-you. No Holy Joe in a starched frock spouting his dust-to-dust crap over a bit of cheap pine. Promise me, girl. I'm counting on...' He stopped. 'What's up? What is it?'

The air, the hot unmoving air, had quivered, and

Midge was staring past him. Following her lead, Juby looked over his shoulder, but only she could see the almost-there boy who stood behind him, a little to one side. The boy saw her too, though evidently not the old man. And the look on his face was so desperately sad that she almost cried out.

Juby darted a questioning glance at her, and when she nodded he did a very odd thing. Having learned where the boy was he turned and walked straight through him, whereupon the lad jumped, like someone woken sharply from a dream, and vanished.

Eighteen

Next morning, following a fitful night of fragmented dreams in which Juby Bench had played a prominent part, there was a letter from Nessa. While congratulating herself for having slipped the Steepridge address through her friend's door before coming away, Midge was surprised to learn the Friedmans were home already until she read why. Nessa's aunt, who lived a few doors down from them, had just been diagnosed with ovarian cancer and needed comforting – especially, Ness confided, since her boyfriend had cleared off a few days before she received the news. All this was delivered in a handful of lines. The rest of the letter was bubbly and chatty, full of the holiday in Wales, what she'd bought, boys she'd seen and fancied – shallow stuff to Midge, whose mind bore a banner headline beside which such news, even that of the aunt's illness, was inconsequential in the extreme:

JUBY'S GOING TO DIE.

Her room wasn't directly opposite his at The Ferryman, but she could see his window well enough to tell if the curtains were drawn. Last night they had been, but now they were pulled back, which meant that he'd probably polished off his Full English and already driven to Rouklye, to start his day there. What a dismal scenario! To go to a particular place to await your death; be terrified of being somewhere else when it came. She picked up Ness's letter again. Reading it a second time might take her mind off Juby. Her eyes skated down the page and fell off the end, having taken nothing in. She returned the letter to the tray Edwin had left outside her door with a discreet knock. Warm rolls and drinking chocolate. Breakfast in bed. They'd never done that before. Perhaps they didn't fancy looking at her miserable mug over the kitchen table.

'Miserable mug,' she said to the mirror. 'Ugly, stinking, miserable, useless mug!'

Mirror Midge glared back at her, clearly agreeing. Non-mirror Midge turned away in despair. There was nothing for it but to sit tight and wait for 'it' to happen.

But then what? Go to Army High Command or whatever they were called, and say, 'Excuse me, chaps, but Juby Bench wants to be buried in Rouklye, follow me, I'll show you where'? Is that the way he imagined it? Did he honestly think they'd listen to her? You had to be off your trolley to believe something like that. Was that it? Was Juby mad? Well, what if he was? He was still someone whose friend she'd claimed to be when pressed, and it was she – she and no one else – that he'd entrusted with his terrible secret. Sometime today, or tomorrow, or the day after, he might sit down suddenly in the schoolhouse or under George V's oak, struggling for breath, and know that this was it. Or, on the track to Crowbarrow under yet another blistering sun, he might keel over and lie there till a range warden drove up and covered his face with a rough Army blanket and radioed for an ambulance. He might even expire in the spiralling, dust-flecked sunlight of the old post office, on the weed-infested floor that smelt of nettles and moss, while visitors took pictures as though death were part of the show.

The worst of it was that there was no one she could talk to about it. Not even Inger. Tears stung her eyes. She dashed them angrily away. Don't be so bloody selfish! Think of someone else for a change. Think of

Juby, who could be dead in days, hours, minutes even. It occurred to her then, out of nowhere really, that she owed him a great debt. A debt like no other. If he hadn't introduced Inger and Edwin all those years ago her mother wouldn't have been born, and if her mother hadn't been born she wouldn't have been either, which meant that her entire existence on this planet was down to Juby Bench. She had him to thank for her very life. And now *his* life was about to end, and she could do nothing for him except hang about in case he came back in a bad way and needed someone there. It wasn't much, wasn't nearly enough, but what else could she do?

So, hour after hour, Midge sat at her window, taking only short essential breaks for fear of missing his return. A long day, long vigil, some of which she passed polishing Larissa Underwood's chess set, moving it over to the window to work on. One by one the pieces came up gleaming, and when she'd finished the whole thing looked a treat, its perfection marred only by the absence of the rook in Juby's pocket.

Her grandparents hardly saw her all day, but they did not intrude or badger her. Edwin fussed a little, worried that something was wrong, but Inger, remembering the oft-thwarted need for privacy in her own childhood, was rather more laid back. 'She's a young woman. Must be sick to the back teeth of us oldies breathing down her neck. Leave her be, Edwin, leave her.'

They couldn't leave her when it was time to go to Jilly Barstow's barbecue, however. When Midge was forced to abandon her post at around 7.50, Juby still hadn't returned.

All day, while Midge sat at her window, gazing vacantly, reading, polishing the chess set, the battered old Volkswagen had stood in Rouklye's sweltering car park. All day, as usual, Juby had wandered here and there, but never far from the village now, never again up steep hills or as far as Crowbarrow. When the hour came for visitors to leave, some time after Midge and her grandparents set out for the barbecue, he folded himself back into his car and drove away, not exactly disappointed to be alive still, but nervous about leaving. Another long night beyond the barriers. If it happened out there, all this would have been in vain.

He was about a mile short of Steepridge when it hit him. A pain such as he'd never known, like a bolt of lightning juddering through him, seeking out every nook and cranny of his being. The car swerved, would have slammed into a tree had he not yanked the wheel back just in time – 'Not yet, you don't, not yet!' – and continued on without a pause. He hadn't come this far to be snatched away before he was ready and in the right place, but he knew he'd just received his final notice. There was no time to waste. He had to get back to Rouklye and stay there till it was over. But first...

Thankfully, the lobby of The Ferryman was deserted, there was no one at the desk, and he was able to get upstairs without being seen. In his room, he boiled the kettle for a flask of tea and packed a small bag with a few provisions. He had no intention of dying of hunger or thirst, whatever else. Then he changed his clothes, thinking, Well, I brought these things, ought to put 'em to use this once. Finally he pocketed the wire cutters he'd forgotten earlier, and slipped back out to the car.

A quarter of a mile from the now-guarded sentry post at the head of the Rouklye road, Juby drove onto a stretch of rarely-used track by an overgrown set-aside field. He got out of the car, gave it a little pat like a faithful pet, then, keeping to cover where possible, set off along a secret way of old which had changed hardly at all over the years. And as the light began to withdraw from this humid August evening, Juby Bench entered Rouklye for the last time, alive.

Nineteen

All three of them had been dreading the Barstows' barbecue, for very different reasons. Edwin dreaded it because he hated large gatherings of people he didn't know, in which he always seemed to spend hours listening to the excruciatingly dull life-story or offensive opinions of someone he wouldn't normally waste a minute on. Inger dreaded it because Edwin got all sniffy when she drank too much, which she intended to do the moment she heard 'You're not English, are you?', which would require her to explain her origins for the ten thousandth time. Midge dreaded it because, apart from not being in a barbecue mood, she expected to be the only non-adult there apart from Henrietta and Nathaniel. Henry was all right, but the prospect of hanging out with her spoilt brother horrified her.

Dread the evening as they might, the three of them stood all-too-soon before a sign –

TO THE BARBIE!

– that told them this was it and they'd damn well better just grit their teeth and get to it. The sign stood at the head of the Barstows' drive, from where they followed a succession of enormous pointing fingers (cardboard) round the side of the house.

Full darkness was almost an hour away, but in the substantial back garden of the Barstow residence, little coloured bulbs already glowed in the trees and bushes near the house. A pall of smoke fanned out from the barbecue, which was tended by Wystan himself, in Hawaiian shirt and white cotton trousers. One of the innocuous country music tapes he kept for gatherings of this kind eased the strained pauses of just-introduced guests, most of whom congregated around the patio. There were a few people Inger and Edwin knew – Steepridgers – but most were out-of-village friends of their hosts, or Army colleagues of Wystan's, several of them still in uniform in spite of the informality of the occasion.

'Didn't know it was fancy dress,' Edwin said, far too loudly.

'Behave yourself,' Inger hissed.

Jilly swept towards them, greeted them with a lot more gush than usual, kissing Inger and Midge on each cheek, Edwin on just one because he shrank from Kiss 2, nostrils flaring against the overpowering musk of her perfume.

Nearby, a broad middle-aged man in uniform stood at the heart of a small but attentive gathering, talking in the fruity, overloud tones of one who assumes that everyone will be fascinated by what he has to say. He had short grey hair and a short grey moustache, and Edwin was much amused by him. 'That's Colonel Legat,' Jilly said, mistaking his expression for one of admiration. 'MoD Conservation Officer down from HQ on a visit. Would you like me to introduce you?'

'I'd rather you introduced me to the beer tent,' Edwin said.

Jilly linked arms with him and Inger and walked them away, either completely forgetting about Midge or assuming she would follow. 'The food will be a while,' she said as they went. 'Wystan had a spot of trouble lighting the coals, but oh, doesn't it smell *wonderful*.'

'Wonderful,' muttered Inger, who had little taste for animal flesh marinated in sweet sauces, then scorched over hot coals. 'Midge,' she called back as they were marched away. Midge moved to follow, but a group of guests to her left suddenly broke up and by the time she got past them her grandparents were just two more heads bobbing round the drinks table – and she was standing face to face with Nathaniel Barstow.

'Oh, it's you,' grunted the Brat without much enthusiasm.

'And you,' Midge replied with even less.

This evening Nathaniel was dressed not in camouflage but, at his father's insistence, in civvies (pressed jeans, neat shirt, polished shoes). He had managed to smuggle out a very authentic-looking pistol, though, and this he raised between them.

'Password!'

'Oh, give me a *break*,' she said, and stepped round him.

The chat was livening up, laughter increasing, as guests relaxed. There wasn't much worth listening to, but when the word 'Rouklye' reached her Midge sought the source, which turned out to be the visiting Conservation Officer. Juby had said something about such a being but she couldn't remember what. She strained to isolate what the colonel was saying from the rising hubbub.

'...affection for the old place...down here whenever I...really got going in the eighties...'

She moved closer, picked up a little more.

'...was a time, in the early days, when our lads took their targets where they found them...anything that didn't move, and probably a few things that...fair to say we've come on a bit since my department was—'

Heavy rock music at full volume suddenly swamped everything. Heads swivelled to the open patio doors, while Wystan dropped his cooking utensils and set off for the house waving apologetic hands and grinning wildly to play down the technical hitch. The music went on for about fifteen seconds, ending as abruptly as it had started, replaced by the indignant shouts of the thwarted Nathaniel. Uneasy chuckles from various quarters, conversations cranking up again, Colonel Legat resuming his monologue.

'...pet scheme of this retired sapper, explosives expert, wanted to create a series of pools for dragonflies. Well, when he'd finished there were these damn great holes all over the shop, but I'll tell you something, the man knew his stuff. Nowadays you can't move out there for the—'

Midge wandered off. About to pass the patio doors, she heard Wystan trying to reason with his errant son inside, urgently and quietly, but not so quietly that she couldn't hear every word as she paused to examine a convenient hanging basket.

'Let me down, Nat, and I'll never forgive you. There are

some important people here tonight and that sort of behaviour does me no good at all. Look, tell you what, be good this evening and we'll take a run into Dorchester next weekend for the record market. What do you say? Just don't show me up tonight, that's all I ask. Deal?'

The Brat must have agreed – silently – for nothing more was said, and shortly afterwards the music started again, not the Iron Maiden that he'd switched to out of devilment, but a muted rhythm-and-blues that was easily talked over. Father and son came out onto the patio and headed for the barbecue, and Midge slipped back into the crowd. Spotting Henrietta across the garden, sitting on a bench with a middle-aged couple, she waved. Henry waved back, looked as if she would like to come over, but couldn't because of the company she was in. Midge cruised, hoping to find her grandparents, who were no longer by the drinks. At one point, finding her way obstructed, she stepped sideways without looking and – 'Whoops, steady there!' – collided with the Conservation Officer. The impact caused the colonel's arm to jerk up and whisky to slop over his hitherto impeccable uniform. A large spotted handkerchief appeared in his hand and he dabbed fretfully at his jacket.

'Dear, dear, dear. Dear-oh, dear-oh, dear.'

'Sorry,' Midge said. 'Sorry, I really am.'

He stopped dabbing. He smiled, his bristly moustache turned up at the ends, and she realised that his audience had disbanded and that she was his new focus of attention.

'Think nothing of it. Accident. Silly place to stand anyway. Guest or resident?'

'Pardon?'

'Were you invited or are you another of the major's...offspring?'

She shuddered at the second alternative. 'Invited,' she answered coolly, deciding, now that her apology had been accepted, that she wasn't all that keen on chatting to men who approved of blowing holes in Juby's valley, even if it was to encourage dragonflies. She would have moved away, but—

'Local, are you?'

'What?'

'Are you from round here?'

'No.'

'Me neither. Hampshire man, based in Surrey.'

For Midge it had been a long and gloomy day in which she'd thought of little but Juby Bench, and that he was going to die soon, in Rouklye if he could manage it. It seemed likely that if the authorities got wind of his plan they would do everything they could to foil it. The authorities. She looked at Colonel Legat; his whisky-stained uniform, his brisk moustache, his small, twinkling eyes. He looked about fifty, which meant that he wasn't even born at the time of the evacuation, but here, now, in that uniform, he represented the force that had snatched Juby's home from him and soured his life when he was just a year older than she was now. But Juby wasn't the only one who'd lost out in that government-sanctioned theft, and it was this, her personal loss, unsuspected until a couple of days ago, that caused a great anger to well up in her, flap in her chest like a trapped bird, and burst out of her mouth in a blind, full-blown fury.

'Just who do you think you are?' she demanded, far too loudly. 'What right have you got to even *be* here?!'

The amiable colonel reeled as though accused of lewd behaviour. 'I...I was invited.'

'Not by *them*, you weren't! *They* didn't invite you! You just barged in and told them to shove off, and now some of them don't even know their own relatives! Wouldn't know each other if they passed in the street, and all because of you and your... your...'

She simultaneously ran out of steam and realised that all other conversation had stopped and that every eye was on her. She clapped a hand over her mouth, but too late.

The damage was done. Inger and Edwin, approaching the scene as this tirade petered out, were among the few who did not look either shocked or amused by what most took for another spoilt kid having a tantrum.

'You know, I think our Midge is coming out of her shell at last,' Inger murmured to Edwin.

'Mm,' said he. 'And we sure know where *she* stands now.'

Iridescent with shame, Midge whirled and fled. The guests parted to let her through. Down the garden she went, desperate to put as much space as she could between herself and the house, the coloured bulbs, the over-loud adults trying to impress one another with their views and choice tones. She heard a shrill laugh, followed by an out-and-out guffaw, and knew they were laughing at her: at a kid putting an Army officer in his place. Her shame was complete.

It was a long garden, with a great many bushes and trees, and as they closed in and the noise receded, she began to breathe more easily, and slow down. It still wasn't quite dark, but the moon was up, and just past full, gently illuminating this shadowy lower end of the garden. She stopped at last, trying not to think what a prat she'd made of herself in front of all those strangers. Her high colour had faded, but even if it hadn't there was no one here to see it unless you counted the rabbits, of which there were three in a large home-made wooden hutch in a small clearing. She glanced at them as they came to the wire to twitch their noses at her, but she wasn't in the mood for rabbits. The hammock now. That was something else.

The hammock, slung between two sturdy trees, was where Wystan Barstow retired to on fine Sunday mornings to read the papers. Midge, imagining herself in it, swinging gently, eyes and senses closed against the world, reached for it. Climbing into a full-size rope hammock is no easy trick for the novice, and this one was such a way above the ground that when she hoiked a foot up into it, it moved away, carrying her with it, the other foot hopping behind, and when it swung back drove her gracelessly before it, this time dragging her grounded foot by the heel. She disentangled herself with some difficulty, steadied the hammock, and tried again, submitting her other foot this time. The same thing happened. She shot forward, then came back, free heel dragging.

'Having trouble, are we?'

Midge jerked round, a sharp movement that caused the hammock to pull away again, yanking her after it, leaving her hanging, one leg in the air. Nathaniel Barstow strolled to the end of the hammock for a better look.

'Knickers,' he leered.

She covered herself as well as she could upside down. 'Shove off!'

The leer widened. 'Shove? You wanna shove? OK.'

Nat the Brat reached across the hammock and tugged, so that it began to sway back and forth all over again, carrying its helpless cargo with it, forward, back, forward, back.

'Don't do that!' Midge said earnestly – but quietly, so her voice wouldn't carry.

'Aren't you enjoying yourself then?' Nathaniel replied, yanking harder to increase the sway. Midge squealed and struggled, but the more she tried to disengage her foot the more entangled it became, forcing her to hop first after the hammock, then before it. Every time it returned, her tormentor gave it another tug or push to keep it going.

'Ah. The little Barstow in action.'

Nathaniel let go of the hammock. Midge gasped with relief.

'Help me!' she pleaded.

'My pleasure,' said Edwin; and to Nathaniel: 'You. Don't move a muscle or utter a sound. Your time has come.'

Nathaniel's muscles obediently froze, though the corners of his mouth dipped a little.

'Can I help?' asked another voice.

Henrietta had witnessed Midge's flight from humiliation; had wanted to follow her and console her but been unable to get away from her uncle and aunt. Only when she saw Nat go after her, and Mr Underwood go after *him*, did she excuse herself and run down the garden. She assisted Edwin in releasing the grateful Midge.

'Now what,' Edwin said then, turning a baleful eye on Nathaniel, 'are we to do with the villain of the piece?'

Although he tried not to show it, Nathaniel quailed before this man, who had never had the slightest patience with the tantrums and bad behaviour that his parents – particularly his doting mother, who seemed to think they were part of his charm – had pandered to all his short life.

'You keep away from me,' he said, attempting defiance.

'Always glad to do that,' Edwin replied. 'However, I think I should take this opportunity to get a few things off my chest before you get much older.'

'What do you mean?'

'Well, for starters, I want to tell you that it's time you stopped acting like a little idiot and learned some respect for others.'

Although considerably short of his eventual height, Nat was at present no taller than the man, but he managed to stand his ground, just. 'Don't get you,' he said, sticking out his lower lip.

'Of course you don't. Why would you? You've never been taught that there are certain ways a person does not behave in public. Because of that you've got away with murder all your little life. But you're fourteen now, with eyes on a military uniform, Gawd help you, and you need to get your act into some sort of order that does not include picking on girls. Now your dear mother will put up with anything you do, however appalling, but unless I'm mistaken your dad is rarely presented with your worst side. Would you say that's true?'

Nathaniel, whose eyes suggested that his preference would be to run back down the garden and bury his face in his mother's consoling bosom, nevertheless managed a moderately insolent, 'What you getting at?'

'This,' said Edwin. 'That if you don't start exercising some behavioural discretion around others – particularly around my granddaughter – I'll blow the whistle on you to your old man.'

'Blow the…?'

'Spill the beans, lad, spill the beans. Tell the major how his son acts up when he's not about, how shoddily he treats guests, how unsuited he is for Army life. And understand this, boy. If there's one more belligerent word or look from you this evening I'll not put off the whistle-blowing or the bean-spilling, in spite of the elevated company. Your father will be presented with the specifics of his obnoxious son's true nature this very night – in front of everyone present. It's up to you. Which way do you want to play it?'

About to offer a bold retort and risk everything, Nathaniel evidently thought better of it, for he stepped back, glanced at the girls as though half expecting them to leap upon him with cudgels, and hurried away.

At the end of the lengthy silence that followed the boy's departure, Edwin said: 'That was a truly horrible performance.'

'Whose?' said Midge.

'Mine. Not my finest moment either. I've never threatened a living soul before, and here I am picking on a young boy.' He turned to Henrietta. 'Sorry, Henry, I shouldn't have said all that in front of you.'

The child agreed. 'No, you shouldn't. You should have videoed it so I could watch it again and again till bedtime.'

'But he's your brother,' said Edwin, amazed.

Henry beamed. 'Don't remind me. You were brilliant.'

TWENTY

Before going to sleep the night of the barbecue, Midge had vowed never to show her face in public again. Unfortunately for her, by the afternoon of the following day more people than she'd ever met in her life were clamouring to see it. It started with a telegram from her mother.

DEAR ALL. WHATEVER YOU HEAR ON NEWS DON'T WORRY. DAVE NOT HURT JUST HELD CAPTIVE. SNEAKY DEVILS BOARDED US IN NIGHT. KEEP YOU POSTED IF I CAN. LOVE MALENA.

'Keep us *posted?!*' Inger shrieked on reading this. 'If she *can?*'

There being no way to reply in order to demand more detail, further information had to be sought elsewhere. Edwin was despatched to the newsagent's along the street. While he was gone, Inger and Midge stared wanly at one another, all sorts of ghastly thoughts running through their minds. Twice in the past Midge's parents, on other missions, had been arrested and put in gaol for a day or two. Once, her dad had been beaten up rather badly by some Algerian soldiers for interfering in their business, but he'd dismissed this as 'par for the course'. Par for the course! In parts of the world, innocent people were losing their heads – literally – merely for being there. She didn't want to *think* what might happen if the Inanians decided to make an example of her non-innocent parents. And it wasn't just them. She knew it was selfish but if Mum and Dad were killed, what would happen to her?

When Edwin came back laden with the day's papers, Inger swept everything off the kitchen table and spread them out. Three pairs of eyes scanned page after rapid page, but came across nothing about the imprisonment of *Earthsave International* activists.

'Malena said their ship was boarded in the night,' Edwin said as they were finishing their search. 'These papers would have been printed before that.'

Inger's eyes widened. 'Why didn't you think of that before we started looking through them? Before you went to *buy* them?'

'Why didn't you?' he said.

She grabbed the papers, threw them on the floor, and jumped on them.

'What about the radio?' Midge suggested.

'You want her to jump on that too?' said Edwin.

'I mean the news.'

'It's forty minutes to the next news.'

'No, I mean ring them to see if they know anything.'

'Good idea,' said Inger. 'What's the number of the local radio station?'

'How would we know?' Edwin said. 'Anyway, it's not a local event.'

'They have news services, don't they? News could be coming in even as we sit here twiddling our fingers.'

'Thumbs,' said Edwin.

Inger rushed to the phone, dialled Enquiries rather than waste time looking through Yellow Pages, scribbled the number she was given, and rang it.

'News desk!' she snapped at the receiver when a voice answered. Then: 'What? No, I don't want a special offer, I want to speak to somebody on the... What are you talking about, I don't have any pets... You're a what?

A vet? What are you doing being a vet, you're supposed to be a radio station... You're not a radio sta...? Oh, *really!*' She slammed the receiver down.

'Try this one,' Edwin said.

He had opened the phone book the moment her confusion started. She looked from the number he showed her to the one she'd written, reversing two digits in her haste – 'Tuh!' – and redialled.

This time she got through, with a negative result: no news had come in about captured *Earthsave* people. Was she sure it wasn't a hoax? Again she slammed the phone down.

'You'll break that,' said Edwin.

She stared at him, frustrated and angry. 'Who else can we try?'

'The newspaper people might have something by now,' Midge offered.

'They might,' Inger said. 'But I think we'll try one of the nationals.' She snapped her fingers impatiently. 'Number, someone, number!'

Edwin picked up one of the papers from the floor. 'Where do I look?'

'Wherever you look, Edwin, look in a different one. All they know about on that rag is tits and bums. We don't want to know about tits and bums, we want to know about Dave.'

She scooped up *The Independent*, found a contact number, and dialled it. 'Good morning! Kindly put me through to the news editor!'

Connected almost at once, she asked her question, and heard that information had indeed started coming in about the *Earthsave* ship. She demanded to be told everything. There was some resistance to this, but she got her way by saying that one of the captives was her son-in-law. Midge and Edwin stood tensely at her shoulder trying to make out what was said at the other end. They got some of it, but far from all. When Inger replaced the receiver, less violently this time, she spelt it out for them in three simple sentences.

'The Inanians have commandeered the 'Boldly Go' and taken off all the men. There was a bit of a scuffle. Some minor injuries but no fatalities as far as they know.'

'As far as they *know?*' Midge squawked.

'What about the women?' Edwin asked.

'They left the women on board. Don't seem to have harmed them.'

'You know why they left the women, don't you?'

'No, why?'

'They knew the first thing they'd do would be to dispatch messages like confetti telling the world what had happened.'

'You mean they wanted them to tell?' Midge said.

'Of course. You don't think they want their security people tied up with loony busybodies like your parents, do you? No, they want the governments of the countries to which the various shipmates are attached, to demand the return of their citizens so they can get on with their tests in peace. I think they'll be delighted to hand them over.'

When they turned the radio on at eleven the bare bones of the story were delivered as a news item. After that, word spread through the area like a bush fire that the couple who ran the Steepridge bookshop were relatives of two of the *Earthsave International* people. Even better, they had the couple's daughter staying with them. People came to goggle, in droves.

'They'll be wanting our autographs next,' Inger growled.

'They're welcome to mine,' said Edwin. 'I always fancied a spot of celebrity.'

Around noon, a three-man TV crew turned up to interview them without prior arrangement. Edwin would also have quite liked to be on telly but Inger would have none of it and demanded to know what right they thought they had, barging in on them at such a time. 'It's news,' the would-be interviewer informed her, and asked if he could film them sitting on the couch flipping wistfully through a photo album. Inger suggested that he depart while he and his crew were still in only three pieces.

By early afternoon the bookshop was more crowded than it had ever been, mainly with summer visitors popping in for a sight of the relatives of an imprisoned *Earthsaver* and his wife. A few bought books as mementoes, but in the end Inger got so fed up with the intrusion that she shooed everyone out, locked the door, and flipped the 'Closed' sign in the faces of those still keen to gawp.

The news didn't change much throughout the day except that the government was reported to be making representations to the Inanians for the release of the four British men, as other governments petitioned for their people. Inger stalked from room to room and up and down stairs, growling under her breath in Norwegian.

'You'd think he was your son, the way you're behaving,' Edwin said.

'Oh, I was forgetting,' Inger snapped in reply. 'Silly me. No relation at all. Thank you for reminding me, Edwin. Now I can relax while they murder my granddaughter's father.'

'*Murder?*' Midge cried.

'Well done, Inger,' said Edwin wearily.

It wasn't until well after a snatched evening meal of bread and cheese, merely picked at, that good news came through on the TV Inger had commanded Edwin (horrified to learn that the game was up) to bring in from the Pottering Shed. The prisoners had been released on the understanding that their governments keep them away from the test area. Inger and Midge howled with relief and ran at one another; danced about like mad things, whooping for joy. Edwin, not given to such displays unless in the guise of someone else, stood watching with a grin.

Only when she'd calmed down did Midge remember Juby. Almost the entire village had popped in during the day – or tried to – plus half the holidaymakers in the region; everyone, it seemed, but him. Juby would surely have come if he'd heard the news. *If* he'd heard.

But if he hadn't...

TWENTY-ONE

Pushing open the door of The Ferryman, Midge saw that the receptionist was the same woman who had directed her to the Breakfast Room on her previous visit.

'I was wondering if Mr Bench was in,' she said when help was offered, hoping that she sounded more casual than she felt.

'Mr Bench?' The receptionist peered over her half-glasses. 'Oh, you were here the other day. You're his...granddaughter?'

'No, but he's a friend of my grandparents across the road.'

'Across the road? Not where all the fuss was today?'

She managed to nod and shake her head at one and

the same time in an effort to forestall further enquiry. 'Is he in please?'

The woman glanced at the board of hooks behind the desk. 'His key's not here, so he could be. I'll see.'

She tapped out Juby's room number on one of the desk phones and put the receiver to her ear.

A voice behind her: 'Hello! Miss Miller, isn't it?' Mr Rackham, bustling out of the TV lounge where he'd been fluffing up cushions for the comfort of residents who might wish to use it.

'Yes,' Miss Miller replied. 'Hello.'

'She's looking for Mr Bench,' the receptionist informed him. 'I'm buzzing him, but there's no answer.'

'I haven't seen hide nor hair of him since breakfast yesterday,' Mr Rackham said.

Midge's heart sank. Juby could have been in Rouklye for the best part of two days and a night, dying, and she hadn't given him a thought for at least half of that time. Some friend!

'Were you supposed to meet him here?' Mr Rackham asked her.

'No, I just thought he...'

She raised her hands from her sides, a small gesture of helplessness that Mr Rackham responded to.

'What say we go take a peek, to put our minds at rest?'

He reached over the desk for the ring of house keys and led the way upstairs. Midge followed with some trepidation. Suppose Juby had come back sometime during the day and was up there still, in bed or on the floor – dead?

About half-way along the first landing Mr Rackham knocked on the door of room 11; waited briefly, knocked again, put an ear to the wood.

'Juby, you there?'

No reply, no sound. He inserted a key in the lock. Midge held back, not wanting to be the first to see. Mr Rackham opened the door a crack, called once more, wary of bursting in on a guest who might not wish to be disturbed. Still no reply. He opened the door further, put his head round, went in.

'He's not here,' she heard almost at once from outside.

She slipped round the half-open door, into a small nothing-much room with nondescript blue and grey wallpaper, a blue washbasin, an over-large walnut wardrobe. A very neat room, very tidy, in which there was nothing of Juby; no sense of him at all apart from the standing suitcase at the foot of the bed. Only his case could be so old and worn and leathery.

Mr Rackham tugged the wardrobe doors open. The wardrobe was empty but for a tangled row of hangers. He glanced at the suitcase. 'Looks like he's all packed and ready for the off. Short visit this year. Thought he'd stay at least to the end of the week since he paid till then – in advance. His idea, not mine.'

As they went downstairs Midge realised what she must do. Crossing the road and entering by the side door she found Inger and Edwin in the kitchen. They were sitting across from one another, an elbow apiece on the table, right hands clasped diagonally as if about to engage in an arm-wrestling contest. A bottle and glasses stood within reach. They were surprised to see her.

'We thought you were up in your room.'

'No, I've been over to The Ferryman.'

'The Ferryman?' Inger dropped Edwin's hand. Edwin sighed; reached for his glass. 'You should have told us. You mustn't go wandering all over the place without telling anyone.'

She closed the door, leant back on it, hands behind her. 'I went to see if Juby was there. He wasn't. Hasn't been seen since yesterday.'

'Well, that's Juby,' Inger said. 'Slips in and out as the mood takes him, always has.'

'Yes, but he didn't sleep there last night.'

'He didn't?'

'No.'

'Well, where is he then?'

'I think he's in Rouklye.'

Inger looked at her watch. 'Oh no, surely not. It must be shut by now.'

Midge pushed herself away from the door and sat down at the end of the table so she could look from one to the other of them.

'Something I've got to tell you.'

And she told them. About Juby's visit to the doctor; about his being given six months to live and surviving into a seventh; about his swearing her to secrecy, and how wretched she felt breaking her promise. The news shook them badly, both of them, but, characteristically, it was Inger who was the first to think of doing something.

'Wystan?' she said to Edwin.

He puffed out his cheeks, considered, then nodded. 'A quiet word in his shell-like rather than a general alert with klaxons and floodlights,' he said. 'Send the troops in in force and the shock alone might kill the old boy. That is if he isn't already...'

He glanced at Midge. She was deathly pale.

TWENTY-TWO

It was admiration for his grandfather's uniform and deportment that had lured James Wystan Barstow into the Army as a young man, though his posting to this area nine years ago had not been one that he'd sought. However, he had settled in easily enough, quietly proud to be following in the footsteps of Major-General Harry Miller, who had ordered the evacuation of the Rouklye Valley fifty-six years ago (though he deemed it socially expedient to keep quiet about his mother's maiden name). The downside of the posting was that so little action went with it that when something like this came up he was more grateful than he cared to let on. Within seconds of Inger's phone call he was on the line to his commanding officer, and once he'd gained permission to proceed had changed back into the uniform that Jilly had hung up for him less than an hour before, and, with his three civilian passengers, drove out of Steepridge at a rate of knots.

Half-a-dozen soldiers and two range wardens were waiting for them by Rouklye pond. Wystan told them to search the village, which they did, quickly and efficiently, reporting back that there was no sign of anyone. They were then ordered to split up and scour accessible parts of the valley within a couple of miles' radius, including the woods, the latter with caution because of the risk of coming upon unexploded shells. As the men were setting off, Wystan reminded them that they were looking for an elderly man who might be in a bad way, and that they were to treat him with all due care and courtesy.

In uniform, Wystan Barstow was a very different person from the cordial Steepridge resident who liked rhythm-and-blues, Hawaiian shirts and barbecues. His back was straighter, his shoulders squarer, and he looked as if a smile would hurt as he leant towards Midge and said: 'I just hope this isn't a wild goose chase, young lady.'

For Midge it had been a day like no other. First her father captured by a foreign power, which might have done anything to him, anything at all; then the realisation that Juby might have died while her thoughts were elsewhere; then the soldiers' fruitless search of the village; now this, Nat the Brat's suddenly officious father daring her to have brought him here on a fool's errand. She dropped her eyes, near to tears.

Inger tapped the uniform on the shoulder.

'Wystan,' she said. 'You may have missed it, but we've been under something of a strain today. We would like nothing better than to put our feet up and shut the world out. We are *not* here for the views – or trying to waste your very valuable time.'

The major flinched. He'd never doubted that Inger Bjølstad could be a formidable woman when crossed. They'd never had a real falling out in all the years of their acquaintance, but he wasn't sure it was worth testing their fragile friendship with something like this.

'No, I realise that, I'm simply saying—'

'Simply say nothing. If Juby isn't here don't you even *think* of blaming Midge. She needn't have said a word to anyone, and what if one of your day-visitors found his corpse tomorrow? What would the media make of *that*, I wonder?'

While Wystan huffed and shuffled his feet, Midge drifted over to Edwin, leaning on the wall by the row of derelict cottages.

'Not much like a film set now, eh?' he said as she joined him.

'Not much. Was that the last time you were here? When you were an extra?'

'Yeh.'

'Must seem quite strange here after all that time.'

'Strange isn't the word,' Edwin said quietly. 'Makes me want to weep.'

'I thought you didn't care about the place.'

He glanced at her. 'Did I give that impression?' His eyes were damp. He looked away again, and, perhaps to distract himself, said: 'This wasn't the only one, you know.'

'The only one?'

'Village they did this to. There was also Little Imber on Salisbury Plain. Similar story. Area overrun by the military, who wanted ever more land, saw their opportunity, told the villagers to get lost, slammed the door in their faces for all time. Same year as here, same month. A relative of mine, Austin Underwood – second or third cousin, something like that – he lived up that way. Spent thirty years campaigning to get Imber returned to the villagers. Didn't manage it.'

'At least he tried,' said Midge.

'Unlike me, you mean?'

'No, I...' She didn't know what she meant.

'Protests rarely work against governments,' Edwin said. 'Might get up the snouts of a few officials, gain a few piddling concessions, but the brass-hats and the politicos always get their way in the end. You think Rouklye's ruined? You should see Imber.'

'Have you?'

'Only in photos.' Then, more to himself than to her: 'I wonder where the old bugger's got to?'

Equally stumped, she looked along the row – and saw, down by King George's oak, the almost-there boy, looking her way.

'Do you think they'd mind if I walked about a bit?' she asked.

'Ask the military man. I'm nobody.'

Returning to Wystan and Inger, she repeated her question. Wystan sucked air. 'Tricky. This is MoD property, and the place *is* closed to the—'

'Oh, Wystan, don't be so stuffy!' Inger cut in. 'The girl wants to take a walk in a perfectly safe area. What do you think she's going to do, ruin the ruins?'

Wystan caved in, but with one proviso: 'Just the village, mind.'

Doing her utmost to appear casual and unhurried, she strolled alongside the wall like one who has all the time in the world. The almost-there boy remained at the tree until she drew near, whereupon he took to the track past the church, flickering a little, like a light that would soon expire. Midge followed him. As she passed the schoolhouse the whispers started; more of them than ever before, rustling unintelligibly, like old leaves nudged by a minor breeze. There was something comforting in the indistinct voices, something companionable that seemed to urge her on. There were also movements at the corner of her eye, the movements of many, but she looked neither to left nor right for fear that the almost-there boy – young Juby Bench – would not be ahead of her when she sought him again.

He halted at the point at which the track narrowed and fell, turned to make sure she was still following, and started down. She got a move on, not wanting to lose him, but his head dropped rapidly below the level of the ground she trod, and by the time she began her own descent he was gone. She no longer needed a guide, however. He had shown her the way. Reaching the foot of the path, she glanced round to ensure that she was not observed, and made for the cordon of tall weeds, irritated with herself for not thinking of this before.

As she parted the tangled barrier the whispers stopped. She saw that the barbed-wire within had been cut and folded back, leaving a clear route through. She stepped forward. The weeds closed behind her with a soft swish. Taking care to avoid nettles and thorns and the flailing ends of the severed wire, she passed into a realm of true and perfect silence, at the heart of which the ruined house of Juby's youth, overhung with ancient trees, rose grey and forbidding in the uncertain evening light.

She moved towards the forlorn shell, dreading what she might find inside.

TWENTY-THREE

The worst of it was that he'd drunk all the tea. For minutes on end, hours maybe – time had ceased to have meaning – this was all he could think about as he sat there on the rubble-strewn floor, head tilted back against the wall, gazing at the darkening blue rectangle above. His strength had ebbed away until he was as weak as a kitten: weaker, for a kitten can jump about and play. In the failing light his mind wandered and it seemed, every so often, as if the sky were a ceiling, and that this was a room furnished with fat armchairs, a sofa, a bulky old sideboard. There was a red and grey floral carpet with a foot-wide gap all round, and chintzy curtains at the windows, and he was a lad again. Over by the fire his bath was waiting, a large tin tub with handles at either end. He saw himself slip off his dressing gown and step in, preposterously tall for his age, sit down quickly to avoid being seen – too quickly, spilling water over the rim. Self-conscious, all ribs and bones and sprouting body hair, he covered himself with the flannel when Mum came in with another pitcher of hot water.

'I don't know what you think you've got to hide, Jube, I've seen it all before, y'know.'

Mum? Two contenders for that title. This one, impetuous, energetic, given to cursing her lot so loudly the neighbours couldn't help hearing, then collapsing in helpless laughter at the absurdity of her situation; the other, more self-contained, who rarely expressed warmth, for him, for life, for anything much. It was the second of these who...

No. Hold on to the best a little longer. She was in the kitchen now, skinning a rabbit for a pie, bottling plum jam, measuring out the ingredients for one of those enormous cakes of hers, stirring the thick fruity mixture with a wooden spoon, in a big brown bowl that he and Edwin would—

No, that wasn't right either. Mum didn't cook. Not if she could help it. She paid someone to come *in* and cook – and to clean, do the washing and ironing, make the fires. She hated household chores, being tied to the home. Frustrated traveller unable to get away because of her domestic situation. No man about the place, no dad, never had been.

Hang on, though. No dad? Course there was. He lived with the sour mother. Like her, he was very lean, with a disapproving mouth, quick with the back-handers, wore a flat cap to work.

Weights pressed down on Juby's eyelids and he was glad to let them close. Easier to see with your eyes shut. See what you want – and remember – block out what you don't.

He was upstairs now, under the blankets. Thick grey bedsocks, hand-knitted by someone or other. The stone hot water bottle was cold, no comfort at all. Birds starting. He eased himself out, took a blanket with him, pulled it up round his ears at the window. Cold early morn, mist breathing on the glass, ghost of a tree just yards away. Mrs Palmer had let herself in the back door. He could hear her downstairs, raking out the kitchen grate. He put his face to the glass to watch her slip out in her crocheted shawl and cast yesterday's ashes across the frosty earth beside the vegetable patch. Back inside now, where she would kneel on the knobbly old hearthrug twisting paper round kindling, light it with a wooden spill, wait till it caught.

He shifted his rump. Hard ground, rough stones. He forced his eyes open. No roof, no wallpapered rooms to wander through at will, no family. Stop kidding yourself, man. Sort your head out. Records should be set straight at the end.

The end.

Air-raid sirens. Horrendous wailing filling the world. Explosions, distant and not so, glass smashing, running feet, shouts of panic – inside as well as out.

'Under the table, Bets! Come on now! You too, boy!'

Head-first into russet chenille, three tall people jostling to share space. His father thrashing about, angry as ever. *'Agh, there's not enough room, specially with longshanks here!'*

'I'll get out then.'

'You stay put.' Dad backed out, stood up, knees creaking. *'I'll sit it out here. They'll be gone soon.'*

'Hector, don't be ridiculous! Come back, we'll make room!'

He flopped into his personal armchair. *'They'll not get me cowering like a whipped dog. Just let 'em try and hit Hector Bench's house!'*

'Oh, don't be so daft! Who do you think's impressed?'

Mum leapt out, ran across the room, seized her husband by the arm to haul him out of his chair and back under the—

Crash.

House next door, blown apart, taking bits of neighbouring houses with it. Bits of theirs.

Peering out through folds of heavy tablecloth, he saw his father half out of the chair, tugged by his lean mother, as the ceiling sagged, opened, disgorged the room above – his own bedroom. They didn't make a sound as it came down, and when the dust settled there wasn't a trace of them. Just a big heap of unmoving debris with his bed on top.

'Juby?'

The sirens went away, the crashes and bangs, the cries from the street. Someone had come in; was coming over, leaning down.

'Juby, you all right?'

'All right – me? Course I am. You?'

'Never better.'

Midge seated herself next to him, leant back, like him, against the wall, took in her surroundings. Stones and scattered bricks; weeds and old leaves; something small and dead over there in a corner: a bird, a rat. Some two-and-a-half yards up, a small brick fireplace set in the wall, and above that nothing but sky, darker than it appeared outside, a canopy between ragged verticals. And stars, just a few as yet, random pinheads in the taut fabric of gathering night. One of them moving, falling to earth. Juby saw it too.

'Shooting star,' he said. 'Get a lot of shooting stars in August.'

'Yes?'

'Known for them, August.'

She felt his sleeve brush her arm. The pale linen sleeve of a jacket she'd not seen him in before. He'd changed his suit for the big death scene. Was even wearing a tie. Nothing fancy, nothing memorable, just a tie to die in. He didn't look right somehow. Not at all himself slumped there against the wall in his best togs.

'Heart's a bit wobbly, Evy.'

'You want me to call someone?'

Eyes instantly sharp. Piercing in the gloom.

'Is there someone with you? I told you to keep it to yourself.'

If he'd had his wits about him, he would have known that she couldn't have come here alone all the way from Steepridge. But she frowned at him; tried to sound offended.

'I said I would, didn't I?'

Satisfied, he sank further into his best summer jacket, which looked even bigger than the black one now. He seemed to be shrinking before her eyes.

They sat in silence after this, wordless and still, she

hoping against hope that no one would call her name, but hoping too that he wouldn't die while she was with him; that they would both get up soon and leave this ruined place, go back to Steepridge together, somehow.

It wasn't to be.

'Tell Edwin,' Juby said after a while, his voice a feeble rasp that she had to strain to hear.

'Tell him what?'

'Tell him... No. He wouldn't listen. But Inger.' He cracked a smile. 'Tell Inger...'

'What shall I tell Inger?' she asked gently.

'Tell Inger I always...'

The last light of the day went out of his eyes, and they closed, very slowly, quite undramatically.

'Juby?'

Nothing.

It was only then that she realised he'd been holding her hand.

She remained there, unmoving, till the sky closed over their heads and she could no longer ignore the voices shouting for her, coming closer, closer. Disentangling her hand from his so-much larger one, his smooth leathery palm, she found something in it. Examined it in the final wink of light. It was his talisman. The fourth chess piece. Juby's rook.

Twenty-Four

The *Earthsave International* activists, though forced to stay out of Inanian waters, had refused to leave the South Pacific. They'd called a press conference to announce that they would remain in the vicinity for as long as the tests were in progress, as observers. If nothing else, they reasoned, this would keep the eyes of the world on the area and perhaps limit Inanian activity to some extent. A telegram from Malena Miller, arriving the evening of this dénouement, ended with:

```
...BUT ALL BEING WELL SHOULD BE BACK IN TIME
TO GET MIDGE HOME FOR COMMENCEMENT OF NEW
SCHOOL YEAR.
```

'Decent of you,' Midge muttered.

She disposed of her parents and the entire South Pacific affair in the opening paragraph of her latest letter to Ness Friedman. In spite of her decision to hold back on additional news so that she would have more to say on her return home, the rest of the three pages dealt in some detail with how she'd led the soldiers to Rouklye to look for Juby; how his young 'ghost' had materialised to show her where he was; how she'd held Juby's hand while he died. But the moment she started reading this back she felt as though she were betraying him a second time by turning him into a story for a friend's entertainment, and tore the letter up. This done, she sat cross-legged on the floor looking through the others she'd not yet posted, and found that so much of what she'd written made her squirm now. In the first letter there were dismissive comments about Steepridge and sarky remarks about the boring old people she was stuck with, and in the others clever-clever asides about the way Juby looked, his nostalgia for the 'old days', his mood-changes, and so on. Disgusted with herself, she tore these up too, and after consigning the pieces to the wastebin set her back against the side of the bed to mull over what Edwin and Inger had told her a couple of hours ago at the kitchen table.

'What do you mean, Juby wasn't from Rouklye?' she'd said when she heard.

'Did he say he was?' Edwin asked. 'I mean actually *say* that?'

'He must have, where else would I have got it from?'

'Well, he wasn't. His mother was. Born there, she was, but when she was a young woman she met Hector Bench (he was a guard on British Railways) and moved up to the smoke with him. Juby was born in a two-up, two-down in Maida Vale.'

'But all his talk of being a boy in Rouklye...'

'Oh, he was no stranger there,' Edwin said. 'His folks didn't have much time for him, you see. They would put him on a train at the start of the school hols from the age of five or six, and Mum and I would meet him at this end. It started as a one-off visit, I believe, but became a regular thing when he responded so well.'

'He travelled all that way on his own at *five?*' said Inger, to whom this detail was also new.

'Or six, not sure. But yes. Can't imagine young kiddies being packed off like that nowadays, can you? Juby loved staying with us. My mum wasn't a cuddly woman, independent as hell, no time for men; but she was open and amusing, and she liked Juby. Saw something of herself in him, I think. But what most clicked for him about Rouklye was all the space and freedom after being cooped up in London with parents who didn't give a monkey's for him. He used to get in a right old state the night before he was due to go home. When Bet and Hector copped it in the Blitz, Mum took him in. Must have been a dream come true for him.'

'A dream that didn't last,' Inger interjected.

'He was beside himself when the eviction notice came,' Edwin said. 'I never saw him so angry. He'd already lost one home and here he was about to lose another. One he was very attached to. He stomped about the valley for days, swearing at the top of his voice. You could hear him shouting a mile away.'

'Where did he go to live when he left Rouklye?' Midge asked.

'With me, initially. In my digs in Wareham. He could have gone with Mum to her brother's in Huntingdonshire. She offered, and Uncle Alaric was agreeable, but Jube didn't want to leave the area.'

'You said he stayed with you *initially*...'

'Mm, couple of months, no more. It was just a bed-sit. Juby had to sleep on the sofa, which was much too short for him. He wouldn't let it go, what had happened to Rouklye. Went on and on about it, drove me barmy. I broke open a fresh bottle of milk the day he moved out.'

'Where did he go?'

'Got himself a room over The Greyhound Inn at Corfe. Worked in the bar to pay for it. He wasn't really old enough, but at sixteen he was well over six-foot and still growing, so he got away with it.'

'I've been meaning to ask,' Inger said to Midge. 'How did you know where to find him at the end?'

She shrugged. 'He'd been trying to cut his way through to the house for days. It was where he most wanted to be.'

'But why that old place?' This was Edwin.

'It was his home,' she said, surprised that he should wonder. 'He was happy there. Yes, I know,' she added when he frowned, 'it was your house, but he did spend all those holidays there, and he did live there with you after his parents were killed.'

'No, he didn't,' Edwin said.

'What? But you said—'

'We didn't live there. No one did in our time. It was always empty, that old place. Boarded up. Wasn't a ruin back then, of course. Still had a roof and a top floor, though the stairs were a bit dodgy. We used to break in, add some artwork to the walls, compete to see who could pee the highest, all the usual laddish shenanigans.'

'Doesn't sound like the Juby I knew,' Inger said.

'Oh, Juby didn't go in for that stuff. Just the village lads.'

'Including you?'

'Naturally. My duty as one of the boys. No, Midge, our house – just a cottage really, semi-detached – was the other direction entirely, up beyond the church. I had a scout round for it when you went off to find Juby. Hardly anything of it now, and easy to miss with all the trees that have grown up around it.'

She was at a complete loss. 'But he called the *other* place his house. He even showed me his bedroom window.'

This generated a bemused hiatus, until Edwin said, very slowly: 'Now that I think of it...'

'What?' Midge said eagerly.

'I'd quite forgotten. He as good as took that old dump over when he moved down in forty-one. Spent a lot of time there on his own, even slept there sometimes – on the floor, there was no furniture. Mum let him get on with it. She approved of independence. I wasn't like that. Not nearly as adventurous as either of them. I think the only time she came close to being proud of me was when I left home at fourteen. Showed initiative, you see. Character.'

'But why would he say he *lived* there?' she persisted.

'I don't think it's so hard to understand,' said Inger. 'A place of his own, furnished from his imagination...'

'He always did have an imagination, old Jube,' Edwin said.

Inger smiled fondly, sadly. 'Yes. He did.'

Then, finally, there'd been the bombshell to beat them all. The admission that explained so much and turned Midge's world on its head. It was Edwin who broached the subject, with:

'There's something else you should know.'

Inger shot an unconvinced glance his way. They had talked about this in private, after Edwin himself raised the matter, insisting that Midge be told. Yet it was Inger, gentled into capitulation by the loss of her old friend, who took up the narrative.

'Another antediluvian tale, I'm afraid,' she began. 'And if it were not told I'm sure no one would be any the worse off; but this fellow has decreed that we must come clean, and I suppose we do owe it to you.'

'What is it?' Midge asked, suddenly nervous.

'You remember my walk with Juby from Amsterdam to Steepridge, and his first visit to Rouklye since the war, and how he was so upset by what he found there that he shot off without a word?'

'Yes...'

'Well, he left me pregnant.'

'He *what?*'

'Yes.'

'You mean – God! – you mean Mum wasn't your only child?'

'No, I don't mean that. Your mother was my only child.'

'Sorry, I don't…'

'She's Juby's daughter,' Edwin said.

'Juby's daugh…' She couldn't finish.

He reached out, touched the back of her hand lightly with a finger. 'You're his granddaughter, Midge. Sad as I am to say it, you're Juby's blood, not mine.'

She stared at him as if he'd just uttered some foolishness typical of old men. 'No. You're my grandpa. Everyone knows that.'

'Everyone *thinks* that,' he said, 'including your parents – and believe me I wish it were true – but, well, there you are. It's a wonder, seeing as Inger's always going on about not giving a fig for what people think, that she agreed to my proposal that she stay in Steepridge and pretend the child was mine, rather than return home and face her family.'

'My father was a strict Methodist minister,' Inger put in. 'If he had learned the truth his outrage would have made my mother's life a misery. She was not a strong woman. The complications of family life, Midge. Take my advice: find a nice cave away from it all and become a hermit.'

There was too much to absorb all at once, too much rearranging of the past to undertake in minutes. Later, later.

'But Juby knew?' she ventured. 'About the baby?'

Edwin shook his head. 'He wasn't around, we had no idea where he'd gone, and by the time he resurfaced Malena was eight or nine years old. Seemed too late to mention it somehow – to him or her.'

'And she doesn't know even now?'

'Only three people in all the world know. The three in this room.'

'Do you think your mum should be told?' Inger asked her.

'I don't know. Do you?'

'I doubt that we'd be doing her any favours, personally. What do you say we leave things as they are? Our little family secret.'

Midge was about to exclaim '*Little* secret!' when there was a knock at the kitchen door.

'Damn, who's that?' Edwin said, rising. He opened the door to Jilly Barstow, who enquired without preamble if

Midge was in. 'Well, she is,' he answered, 'but this isn't the time to seek her kid-sitting services.'

'That's not why I'm here,' Jilly said.

'Come in,' Inger said, and, when she did: 'Oh – not alone, I see.'

Skulking rather timidly in his mother's wake was Nathaniel, and, peeking round him, plainly keener to be here, little Henrietta. As they entered it escaped no one's notice that Henry carried a bouquet of flowers so enormous that she needed both hands to wield it.

'Oh, you should have,' Edwin said.

'They're not for you,' said Jilly.

Henry went to the table and, beaming, held the flowers out to Midge.

Midge stared. 'What's this?'

'They're for you,' said Henry.

'From all of us,' her mother elucidated. 'In recognition of what you did.'

Midge stood up, puzzled. 'What I did?'

'Leading Wystan to poor Mr Bench. He wanted to apologise for doubting you.'

'Pity he couldn't do it in person,' Inger muttered.

'This isn't necessary,' Midge said, locking her fingers behind her back.

'I think it is,' said Jilly, unintentionally revealing that

both the bouquet and the apology were her idea. 'And Nat wanted to come too.' She turned to her son. 'Didn't you, Natty?'

Nathaniel, shifting from one foot to the other, was unable to meet Midge's eye for more than half a second at a time, though he seemed to want to. She understood his discomfort, and believed that he really had asked to accompany his mother. His presence was his way of showing that her action at Rouklye had earned his respect – on a take-it-or-leave-it basis, of course.

She accepted the flowers because they could not be refused; graciously enough if without much pleasure. The gift of them reminded her of something she'd been trying to put out of her mind: that she'd been with Juby only for the last few minutes of his life, when he might have been glad of her company for longer. So little time to spare a dying friend. The flowers, though well-intentioned, amplified her remorse.

TWENTY-FIVE

The fourth rook was back where it belonged – not in Rouklye, where it hadn't originated anyway, but on the now-gleaming chess board in her room. She hoped Juby would have forgiven her for this if he'd still been about. Feeling that she ought to know a bit about the game after all that had happened, she had borrowed a *Chess For Dummies* from the shop, from which she learnt that each piece had a function of its own. King, queen, knight, bishop, rook, pawn, they all moved in different ways around the board. The rook's moves – surprisingly, given that Juby had carried one with him for so long – were among the most direct, travelling only in straight unimpeded lines, horizontally or vertically, until it reached a square occupied by an opponent's piece. As

237

a symbol of Juby's life and character it didn't work. She doubted that he'd ever been much of a one for strict rules or straightforward advancement, though he'd certainly had a single-minded objective at the last.

She was again sitting on the floor of her room when she got that prickly feeling of not being alone. She glanced to her right, half-expecting to find the almost-there boy waiting to be noticed. But it wasn't the almost-there boy, it was her own reflection in the chevalier. She got to her feet. So did Mirror Midge. They advanced, and each spread the fingers of one hand on the glass, the right hand of one, the left of the other; touched fingertips. Each studied the other's face. *Rare birds, you and me, Evy. Rare birds.* Rare as in unusual, she thought. Out of the ordinary. I am an unusual, out-of-the-ordinary person. Not like anyone else, anywhere. Well, just one. The gawky awkwardness, the ratty hair, the big nose, they made sense now. 'Thanks a lot, Juby Bench.' But she smiled as she said this.

She dropped her hand. So did Mirror Midge. But when they stepped away, the real Midge Miller was the one who did not live in a mirror. And as she went out to the landing and started downstairs she knew something else: that when she was back home, telling Ness about everything that had happened (editing and highlighting where necessary, of course) it would be she, the Midge who'd stepped back from this side of the mirror, who, just for once, would be the one to envy and point out proudly to friends.

Inger and Edwin had been on the point of arranging a small service for Juby in Steepridge church when Midge told them of his horror of such an event, and his request to be taken to Rouklye. Inger at once approached the authorities, but was refused permission to bury him in the churchyard. No one had been buried there for years and they weren't about to make an exception for someone who'd lived most of his life abroad. But they agreed to allow his ashes to be scattered there at an appointed time, after the day-visitors had gone.

So it was that on a fine August evening a sturdy grey urn was carried to Rouklye in a scuffed leather satchel that had belonged to Edwin's mother. Army representatives and soldiers kept a discreet distance while the small group gathered around the spot to which Midge directed them: the patch of grass Juby had claimed for himself with the stamp of a sandaled foot. Five of the mourners were Juby's family, who'd come over from Germany after Inger phoned with the tidings. Midge hadn't had much to do with the Müellers since their arrival that afternoon. There'd been so little time, and besides, conversation was far from easy. Juby's daughter Johanna spoke good English, but her husband's was very limited and the two girls, if they knew any, did not attempt it. Edwin, like Midge, spoke no German, but Inger could get by in it, so, when necessary, she did the talking for them. The third child, the boy, was studying English at school and was fluent enough, in a stilted sort of way, though he seemed to want to keep himself to himself. Midge had difficulty keeping her eyes off Juby Müeller. He was his grandfather to the life, exceptionally tall, with the same bushy hair, but dark brown rather than grey. He even had the same nose, though fortunately for him it wasn't as developed as the old man's. Even more disconcerting than his features, however, was that every now and then she caught him staring at her with bright blue eyes. The stare was that of the almost-there boy.

Edwin asked if he might be the one to scatter the ashes. 'We were close in our day,' he said. There were no objections. He emptied the urn very carefully over the chosen spot, in a slow arc so that a heap would not form. Midge found it hard to believe that that long streak of a man could be contained within such a modest vessel. Edwin slapped the pot two or three times to dislodge malingerers, which shot forth, whirled in a hesitant final dance, and expired on the short springy turf with the rest. Midge wondered what was wrong with her. Shouldn't she be more moved by all this, or sadder, or – something? She glanced at the others to see how they were affected. Although Edwin's brow was more furrowed than usual, his expression was otherwise unreadable as he stared at the ashes he'd deposited. Juby's fair-haired granddaughters looked rather bemused by the whole business, but on their mother's cheek there was a single slow tear. Their father stood straight-backed throughout, appropriately solemn, while the boy stood apart from everyone, avoiding all eyes. Only Inger turned away so that her face could not be seen, shoulders shaking silently.

And then an odd sensation came over Midge. Whether it was the slanting evening sunlight or the mood of the occasion she couldn't have said, but she felt a small warm shiver, and suddenly there seemed to be nine of them there – nine where there should be eight. She counted, and eight there were, but the feeling persisted that another now stood among them. She touched Inger's arm.

'Would it be all right if I went down there for a minute?' She gestured in the direction she wanted to go.

'I'll ask.'

Glad of the distraction, Inger hastened to the steps, where a captain leant against the gate waiting for them to finish so his men could soak Juby's ashes into the ground with watering cans. Midge met her half-way as she returned.

'Permission granted – as long as you don't go in this time.'

'I won't.'

In the few days since Juby's death – perhaps as a result of it – most of the weeds this side of the house had been hacked down. The warning signs were still there, more visible than ever, and the repaired wire fence; but for the first time she had a clear view of the ruin from outside the barrier. She stood gazing at it without really focusing, her thoughts not on the house particularly, or anything else she could put a name to, but in no-man's land, no-Juby land, no-Midge land; so adrift in nothingness that when the silence was suddenly punctured by a harsh cry, followed by a frantic high flurrying, she returned to the present, and the place, with a cruel bump. Looking up, she saw a large black bird leap from the dense foliage. Free of the trees, the rook soared, twisted and tumbled through the air, as though performing for her benefit.

'Juby,' she breathed.

And, from behind her: 'Yes?'

She whirled round. Stared up at the tall, thin figure standing at the top of the rise. 'You made me jump!'

Young Juby Müeller, at once full of apology, managed, in his precise, serious way: 'I thought you spoke my name.'

'No,' she said. 'What do you want?'

'I wondered where you were going.'

'You *followed* me?'

'Well, I...' Painfully shy at the best of times, it had taken courage for him to go after her, particularly as he considered his command of her language so inadequate. 'I am sorry,' he said, and turned to go.

'No, wait,' Midge said. 'It's OK.'

He stopped. 'Are you sure?'

'Yes. Stay.'

He relaxed a little, but did not yet complete his descent. 'What is that building please?' he enquired politely.

'What building?'

There was only one in the immediate vicinity, but she needed time to think what to tell him.

'That one, that... ruin.'

She decided. 'It was your grandpa's house.'

He virtually gaped. 'That is where he *lived?*'

'It's where he died,' she nearly said, but stopped herself just in time. Instead: 'Yes.'

Juby Müeller, excited, enthralled, no longer inhibited, almost jumped down the path.

'But it is so *different*,' he said, halting at the bottom, eyes raking the decapitated building.

'Different?' She looked up at him. He really was very tall for his age. 'Have you seen an old picture or something?'

'No, I...' She waited. 'I...' Whatever it was, he did not find it easy to express or explain. 'I... dreamed it,' he confessed at last.

'Pardon?'

'I dreamed of the whole village. And none of it was like this.'

'Like this?'

'Ruined.'

Midge took a long, slow breath. 'Tell me about your dream.'

'There were a number of them,' he replied. 'They started shortly after Großvater left. I dreamt of walking here, and of being inside the little school, and of a path to the sea. In one dream I stood on high cliffs and watched a terrible storm.'

'Were there any people in your dreams?' She tried not to sound too interested.

'I saw only one,' he said.

'Your grandfather?'

'No. I was aware of him, but he was always not quite present. I sensed a great pain in him. In the final dreams I knew he was going to die.' He glanced again at the ruined house. 'And where.'

'Who was it you saw in these dreams if not him?' Midge asked.

He looked from the house to her. 'Who?' She waited. And then, quietly, almost with embarrassment: 'You.'

'Aaah.'

So there it was. As it had been all the time. The almost-there boy hadn't been Juby Bench's younger self, he'd been Juby Müeller dreaming of the Rouklye his grandfather had described so often, in such fond detail. When he had walked here in his dreams, this boy had seen not a pitiful huddle of unroofed buildings and fenced-off woods presided over by the military; he'd seen the beloved haven of a storyteller's youth. And he had encountered just one person. An unknown blood-cousin.

'Did we speak in your dreams?'

Juby Müeller shook his head. 'I tried to talk with you, but no words came, and I could not hear you.' He attempted a wry smile. 'But here you are, in real-life. No dream. Crazy stuff, huh?'

Crazy. Oh yes. What could be more crazy than your dream-self walking around a place you'd never visited – as it was in its heyday – and being seen by non-dreamers in broad daylight? One non-dreamer anyway. But was it any crazier than ghosts, magic, belief in a supreme supernatural being?

She looked again at the house in which Juby Bench had taken his final breath while holding the hand of the granddaughter he didn't know he had.

'You see that window up there?' She pointed. 'That was his bedroom. He told me he used to wake up as it got light and lie there listening to the dawn chorus.'

It wasn't quite what he'd said, but she wanted to give the boy something to carry with him as this sad day receded into his past. Young Juby frowned, not quite understanding 'dawn chorus', but was then lost again in the remains of the old building that rose up before him.

'When I am at home in Wiesbaden I will see him at that window.'

'So will I,' Midge said softly. 'When I'm back in Worcester.'

The rook that had returned to the village cawed once more to rebuke them for ignoring it, then sank back into the trees: the nest it had made.

'Midge! We have to go!'

Edwin stood at the top of the path.

'Coming,' she said.

He turned and headed back. She started up the slope.

'Midge?' Juby Müeller said, following. 'Is that your real name?'

'Why wouldn't it be?'

'I wondered, that's all.'

'My proper name's Evy. But Midge is what I'm called. Usually.'

'I like Evy,' Juby Müeller said. 'Good name.'

She glanced over her shoulder, down at him. Was he making fun of her? The look on his raised face seemed to belie that. She continued her ascent, and as she did so heard a number of voices from beyond the rise. Reaching the top, she saw, in the mellow evening light, men who hadn't been there before leaning on garden walls that also hadn't been there, and women tutting kids, others chatting to neighbours. Houses and cottages had roofs and doors, there were curtains at windows, flowers in gardens, cats on ledges, dogs mooching by gates. Rouklye was whole again, and occupied not by military forces but by ordinary people living the kind of lives that had been lived here for generations. Then came the birdsong, oceans of birdsong, enough to fill all the woods of old Rouklye. A perfectly-staged scene, as flawless as an old man's rose-tinted picture of a bygone age. But it was also, somehow, as though the ruins and the soldiers and the tanks on numbered hillsides were the unreality; that this was the way things should be.

And then it was gone, all of it: the chirrups and whistles of the birds; the cosy chatter of the people; the flowers; the animals; the curtains; the roofs. Silence returned, along with the soulless ruins, deep in weeds, laden with ivy, crouching in the casual shadows of antique boughs.

'Did you see?' she whispered as Juby Müeller joined her at the top of the path. 'Did you *hear*?'

He said nothing, but as they walked past the schoolhouse to join the others waiting by the King's oak, Midge glanced slyly at him. A faraway look had crept into his pale blue eyes; a look she knew very well indeed. And there was a trace, she noticed, just a trace, of a smile on his lips.

AFTERWORD
by Evy Miller

I went back to Rouklye recently, some years after the events described here. Another sweltering August day. Nothing much had changed. The valley was still MoD property. The woods were still out-of-bounds. There were still warning notices and barbed-wire fences at every turn.

Most of the ruins were still as they had been too, though a few had been partially rebuilt and made accessible. I took one of these to be the semi-detached cottage where Edwin had grown up and Juby had spent his holidays and gone to live for a couple of years before the evacuation. A display board showing four photographs stood in front of the building. The first picture, the only one in black-and-white, showed it as it was in the early 1940s, double-storeyed, a tiled roof, two small gated gardens, washing on a line. In the next, dated 2005, all that remained were bits of crumbling lower wall draped with brambles, while in the third photo, taken two years later, the structure was surrounded by scaffolding, with the walls a bit higher. In the final picture it was as it appeared today – still no roof, doors or windows, no hint of any gardens, but with the walls rebuilt to the first floor. Below the photos there was this printed message:

These cottages have been partially renovated for general viewing at a cost of £55,562, which funds have come from church sales and public subscription. Please treat the building with care.

ARMY IN CO-OPERATION WITH THE PUBLIC

I could think of a couple of people who, if they'd still been about, might have seen the irony of this. The occupants of a pair of perfectly good cottages had been evicted with the approval of a democratically-elected government and their homes allowed to crumble by the new owners, who, many years later, were accepting public donations for a token rebuilding scheme to show that their hearts had really been in the right place all along. I could almost hear Edwin's dry chuckle – probably in someone else's tones – and Juby's hoot of derision.

From there I climbed the steps to the churchyard, where I stood for a minute or two by the patch of grass on which we'd scattered Juby's ashes. After that there were just two places to revisit.

The photo of the children who'd attended the school in 1912 still hung in the little cloakroom, and beyond, in the vaulted classroom, oil lamps still dangled from the ceiling. The piano was also still there, and the rows of linked desks, the blackboard on its easel beside the fireplace – though with different information and suggestions as to what to look for outside. Rookeries were mentioned.

Leaving the schoolhouse, I took the path down to the last building I had to see, where I found that the woods had been cut right back and the barbed-wire removed. The old house looked much the same from the outside, but work had been done to make it safe to enter. Anyone could wander into it now. I didn't like that much. It didn't seem right that strangers could stroll around Juby's adopted home. I could have gone in myself, but I knew that if I did I would see him sitting on the rubbled ground in his best suit, feel his dead hand in mine, and his cherished talisman.

I turned away. But as I turned I thought I caught a movement in the upper reaches of the building. I squinted up through a shaft of rusty sunlight and saw a tall figure gazing out from one of the window spaces. I blinked, and he was gone, and I decided that the ancient light of Rouklye had played one of its tricks on me. But as I was leaving that place forever, never to return, I gave that empty window a little wave, in case I hadn't imagined him.

Juby Bench. My friend. My grandfather.

MIDGE MILLER'S FAMILY TREE

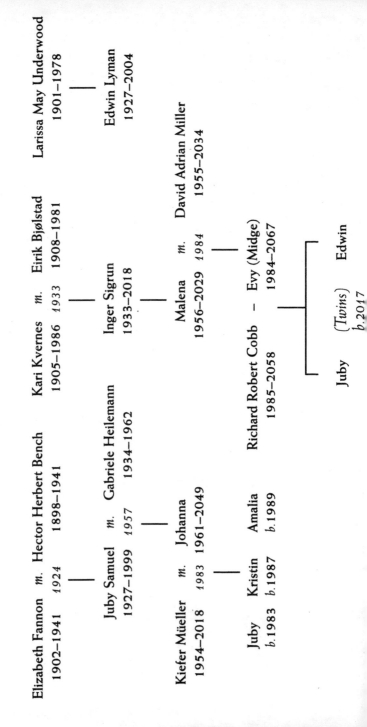

Elizabeth Fannon *m.* Hector Herbert Bench   Kari Kvernes *m.* Eirik Bjølstad   Larissa May Underwood
1902–1941   *1924*   1898–1941   1905–1986 *1933* 1908–1981   1901–1978

                                                                                      Edwin Lyman
                                                                                      1927–2004

          Juby Samuel *m.* Gabriele Heilemann   Inger Sigrun   David Adrian Miller
          1927–1999 *1957*   1934–1962   1933–2018   1955–2034

                                                        Malena *m.* Evy (Midge)
                                                        1956–2029 *1984* 1984–2067

Kiefer Müeller *m.* Johanna   Richard Robert Cobb – Evy (Midge)
1954–2018 *1983* 1961–2049   1985–2058   1984–2067

Juby   Kristin   Amalia   Juby   *(Twins)*   Edwin
*b.*1983 *b.*1987 *b.*1989   *b.*2017

ORCHARD BOOKS YOU MAY ENJOY

Ten Days to Zero	Bernard Ashley	978 1 84362 649 7
Down to the Wire	Bernard Ashley	978 1 84616 059 2
Flashpoint	Bernard Ashley	978 1 84616 060 8
Little Soldier	Bernard Ashley	978 1 86039 879 7
Revenge House	Bernard Ashley	978 1 84121 814 4
Tiger Without Teeth	Bernard Ashley	978 1 84362 204 8
Tag	Michael Coleman	978 1 84362 182 9
The Cure	Michael Coleman	978 1 84616 345 6
Weirdo's War	Michael Coleman	978 1 84362 183 6
Jacob's Ladder	Brian Keaney	978 1 84362 721 0
The Hollow People	Brian Keaney	978 1 84616 225 1
A Crack in the Line	Michael Lawrence	978 1 84616 283 1
Small Eternities	Michael Lawrence	978 1 84362 870 5
Milkweed	Jerry Spinelli	978 1 84362 485 1
Stargirl	Jerry Spinelli	978 1 84616 600 6

All priced at £5.99

Orchard books are available from all good bookshops, or can be ordered direct from
the publisher: Orchard Books, PO BOX 29, Douglas IM99 1BQ
Credit card orders please telephone 01624 836000
or fax 01624 837033 or visit our website: www.orchardbooks.co.uk
or e-mail: bookshop@enterprise.net for details.

To order please quote title, author and ISBN
and your full name and address.
Cheques and postal orders should be made payable to 'Bookpost plc.'
Postage and packing is FREE within the UK
(overseas customers should add £1.00 per book).

Prices and availability are subject to change.